Who was THE SCARECROW?

Was the country parson, Dr. Syn, really the leader of a band of smugglers? John Banks, the judge's son, knew for sure. But he was sworn to secrecy, just like all the "Gentlemen" who were helping the poor of England pay the taxes of the king.

Follow the exciting adventures of Doctor Syn alias THE SCARECROW in a super book based on the Walt Disney movie.

DR. SYN
ALIAS
THE SCARECROW

Vic Crume

TEXT ILLUSTRATIONS BY JOSEPH GUARINO

From the Walt Disney Productions' film, screen-play by Robert Westerby and based on the book, *Christopher Syn,* by Russell Thorndike and William Buchanan.

PYRAMID BOOKS ▲ NEW YORK

DR. SYN ALIAS THE SCARECROW

A PYRAMID BOOK

Cover illustrations and text
Copyright © 1975 by Walt Disney Productions

Pyramid edition published November 1975

ISBN 0–515–04045–2

Library of Congress Catalog Card Number: 75–29975

Printed in the United States of America

Pyramid Books are published by Pyramid Communications, Inc. Its trademarks, consisting of the word "Pyramid" and the portrayal of a pyramid, are registered in the United States Patent Office.

Pyramid Communications, Inc., 919 Third Avenue, New York, N.Y. 10022

CHAPTER 1

... From the marsh to the coast
like a demon ghost ... through the
black of night he rode. ...

High on the curving line of sand dunes, three
hideously-masked horsemen reined up their powerful mounts.

The leader of the trio chuckled hoarsely. "Cloudy
night, calm sea. Scarecrow weather, my lads!"

5

No wonder all England called that gaunt figure astride the mighty iron-gray stallion "Scarecrow." His painted gunny-sack mask was frightful. From the straw wisps that poked out beneath a raggedy hat to the shoulders of the great black cloak he wore draped over the length of a broomstick—scarecrow he seemed to be.

The two riders at his side nodded. It was true. A pale moon cast hardly enough light to sparkle the wavelets frilling the shore. Only a few bobbing lanterns just off the beach showed that, once again, the French Captain and his men were already in their rowboats. With every pull on the muffled oars, the sailors were bringing closer to shore the smuggled cargo so dear to the heart—and even dearer to the purse—of England's King George the Third.

"With sharp lookouts—and a little luck—" the gaunt horseman on the mighty gray murmured, "the King's soldiers will fail this night to collect the King's taxes."

Even in the dim light, the mask he wore was so terrifying, it frightened foe and friend alike. No one but Hellspite and Curlew, his two trusted companions, knew his true identity. Yet he commanded the loyalty of a band of over one hundred men waiting at the waves' edge to unload the small boats launched from the French clipper anchored far offshore. They stood ready with heavy farm carts and sturdy ponies to take on the precious cargo of casks

and bales—though it would be death by hanging to any man caught.

The men were farmers turned smugglers. Honest country folk who loved their land. But bled to the bone by a mad king's harsh tax laws, their loyalties now turned to the one they called "Scarecrow." He it was who had found for them the way and means to pay those cruel taxes. He would keep thatched cottage roofs safe over their poor heads!

But these same men, brave enough to face the hangman's noose—or a long sentence at the king's prison in nearby Dover—shuddered at the very sight of the Scarecrow. They held their breath in fear as the three masked riders galloped their horses down the dune slope to the sea's edge. To the smugglers, the Scarecrow and his two lieutenants seemed to be three horrible demons riding out of the marshlands—fiends out of darkness pounding ever closer. And not a man among them would fail to obey the Scarecrow's commands!

Now their horrifying leader guided the iron-gray past the line of carts and ponies and went on to the last boat being pulled ashore.

"Load up and on your way, lads," he urged. "We'll tweak King George's nose, never fear! And a tweak it will be with every cask and every bale."

The French captain, Capt. Delacroix, was as anxious as the Scarecrow for the last of the unloading to be done. He looked uneasily seaward. "Come on men! Hurry, or I'll lose the tide!"

He turned as Scarecrow guided the big iron-gray forward. "That's the whole cargo, M'sieur Scarecrow."

Scarecrow nodded. "Your payment, Captain." He tossed down a money bag.

The Captain caught it and bowed. "We will be—"

A shouted warning from far up the beach cut short his words. "Horsemen on the sea road, Scarecrow!"

Almost at the same moment, a second lookout posted even farther away swung his lantern in warning.

Scarecrow wheeled his horse about. "Douse all lights! Go! You all know your orders, lads. My lieutenants, Hellspite, Curlew—follow me!"

With a horrible roaring laugh, and hardly before the sailors could step back into the boats, nor the smugglers move the creaking carts, Scarecrow and his lieutenants pounded back up the dune slope. They pulled their mounts to a halt. A sudden gust of sea breeze caught at Scarecrow's witchlike black cloak. And as it billowed out, the iron-gray reared nervously.

"Steady! Steady!" Scarecrow's gloved hand stroked the powerful dappled neck. "Save your strength for the run you shall have!"

Hellspite and Curlew well knew what the "run" would be. If the riders on the sea road proved to be the King's soldiers, that run would be a race. And a purposely close race, at that! To keep the soldiers away from the slow-moving line of carts and ponies on the beach, the three must lure them landward. This meant they must not too far out-race their pursuers, but stay within sight until that one last moment. And that last moment was Scarecrow's to command! Even now, their hands tightened on the bridles as they waited for the hoofbeats on the sea road to come closer.

Scarecrow lifted his hand. "Hark!" He listened. "We'll be evenly matched, lads! Three of them, I'll warrant."

As the riders drew near, Scarecrow dug his heel against the iron-gray's flank. The big stallion snorted and reared forward, square in the path of the oncoming soldiers.

"It's him!" came a shout. And the leader, a captain, nearly jolted out of the saddle as his mount swerved.

"The Scarecrow!" his two companions shouted.

Like three streaking witches, cloaks flying, Scarecrow, Curlew, and Hellspite bolted off across the sea road and on into the wild countryside.

"After them!" the captain yelled. And hard on the heels of the fleeing horsemen, the King's men raced, firing their pistols desperately.

Over boulders, over bushes, around boulders, around bushes, the Scarecrow held a dizzying, galloping pace. Then suddenly, in a mad straight-away dash, the three put their horses over a low fence.

Ahead, and up a sloping lane, stood the ruins of an old castle and ancient barn. Rough rock walls showed gray against the sky, and wide black spaces appeared where once had stood sturdy oaken doors.

Straight into the ruined castle rode Scarecrow and his men. And straight out the far side! On to the old barn they raced—and vanished.

· But at the castle's ruined walls, the captain halted his men. "We have them now!" he shouted. "Circle, men!"

Minutes later, the soldiers knew they had lost their quarry—unless, *unless* they were hiding in the ruined barn.

Quickly they dismounted, stalked forward, pistols drawn.

"Nobody's hiding in here, sir," the corporal reported a moment later. "But for a bit of hay it's bare as a bone."

"So I see," the captain replied icily. "But they *must* be around. We'd have seen them if they'd gone on. What were they? Ghosts?"

"Oh, no, sir. They were real enough."

"We'll search the place again," the captain snapped. "Carefully!"

But even though three men *could* be hiding in some dark corner of the old barn, good sense forced the captain to admit that three big horses could *not*. He stared down at the loose hay that littered the old floor. "All right, men," he called disgustedly. "We'll give it up. There's nobody here."

Fortunately for Scarecrow, Curlew, and Hell-

spite, the good captain was no more able than
anyone else to see through solid oak flooring. It
formed the ceiling of Scarecrow's underground
stable hideaway. Hands over the noses of their
steeds, the three masked men waited, hardly daring to breathe.

"They're gone," said the wild figure standing by
the iron-gray. He stroked the big horse's muzzle.
"Good fellow!" he said softly. "You wouldn't give
Scarecrow away by one whicker, would you?"

He then peeled off his hideous mask, revealing a
handsome smiling face. "Nor would you give away
the Vicar of Dymchurch either, I guess."

His companions, too, jerked off their masks. The
taller and much older of the two grinned. "If he
had, it would have given your parishioners a fine
shock, Vicar. You, their pastor, scampering about
the marshlands in the dead of night!" He stepped
forward to help the vicar remove a broomstick
from the shoulders of the scarecrow cloak.

Doctor Christopher Syn, Vicar of Dymchurch,
once again looking like the kindly, normal, human being the villagers were used to seeing,
grinned back. "Thank you, Mipps." He settled his
cloak back into place. "And have you thought of
the villagers' shock if they knew their sexton who
rings the church bell, tends the church, and—"

"Builds the coffins," Mipps, the sexton, inter-
rupted cheerfully. "Yes, it would come as a surprise,
indeed."

His face turned suddenly solemn. "It's building *your* coffin that worries me, sir. Happier I'd be if you'd throw away that Scarecrow mask forever—before your luck runs out."

"Before his *luck* runs out?" an indignant voice cried.

Both the vicar and the sexton turned in surprise and stared at the third, and by far the youngest member of their trio—John Banks, second son of wealthy landowner, Sir Thomas Banks. Sir Thomas was justice-of-the-peace and judge at trials in the little village of Dymchurch-under-the-Wall. He would have been horrified if he could have seen or heard his son that moment.

John's bright, dark eyes were snapping. "Luck, you say. It's Dr. Syn's skill, Mipps. He plans. He *thinks*."

"And a good thing it is that your father doesn't know what our vicar plans and thinks, Master John," Mipps replied good-naturedly. "He might never let you out of the manor house."

John's eyes saddened. He shrugged. "Father scarce notices I'm even there. His thoughts are always about Harry. Sometimes I think he doesn't know he ever had another son."

Dr. Syn laid a hand on his young friend's shoulder. "Your poor father," he said sadly. "To lose Harry in such a way! But come now! It grows late. We'd best be where we're expected to be at such an hour. I'll ride out. Give me five minutes. If you hear no shooting, you'll know all is well,

and it will be safe to follow. Old Mother Hathaway will take care of our horses. Don't worry, either of you. They're probably miles away from here by now."

Mipps shook his head. "It's not the smuggled cargo they're after, sir. It's the reward money for your capture."

"Well, Mipps, let's not worry about that. We'll saddle old Fatty for my journey back, no one is likely to suspect an elderly pony of chasing about the marshes at night."

As the vicar led a fat, gray pony along the sloping tunnel leading to the secret entrance, Mipps and John hurried ahead to open the trap door.

Then mounting up, Dr. Christopher Syn, Vicar of Dymchurch, started off through the night at a sedate, jogging pace.

It would never have entered anyone's head that the calm, handsome face beneath a vicar's hat—hidden beneath a hideous mask—was being shown on hundreds of posters along the south coast of England.

> THE SCARECROW,
> REWARD.
> ONE THOUSAND POUNDS IN GOLD.
> ALIVE OR DEAD.

But Dr. Christopher Syn, kindest and most gentle pastor the villagers had ever known, was an angry fighter for human justice. And he fought in a way King George the Third of England would gladly punish by death!

CHAPTER 2

Dr. Syn was not the only person eager to reach the village. About two miles behind him, a big stagecoach lumbered along toward Dymchurch.

Three of its four passengers swayed, joggled, and hoped it would not be much longer before the village came into view. But the fourth, slumped in his corner, eyes closed, was seemingly fast asleep.

Far from sleeping, Simon Bates, rumpled and exhausted, was wondering if he'd ever again see the beloved land he'd left an ocean away from England.

"At least I'm alive," he thought wearily. "And that's more than I'd thought possible last night."

Only that morning, in a foggy dawn, he'd escaped certain death in Dover Castle prison. Sick with fear, he'd walked the old streets, sure that any moment he would be caught and returned to that place of doom. But he knew it would not be safe to strike out into the countryside while it was still daylight.

By late afternoon, hungry, thirsty, footsore, Simon's luck changed—and at the very door of a busy Dover inn! A kindly-looking gentleman, dressed in the garb of the Church, stepped from the inn entrance and into a waiting stagecoach. "Do you wait for the Dymchurch stage?" he called from the window. "If so, you may share my conveyance. I go to that village myself."

Simon mumbled his thanks—and to no less a personage than the Archbishop of Canterbury on his way to conduct services in Dr. Syn's church!

"You appear ill," the kindly archbishop said as Simon leaned back in the corner.

"Only weary," Simon smiled faintly.

And then the worst happened! Hardly had he settled back than the archbishop again called out the window. This time to two travelers stepping from the inn. They, too, were invited to share the coach.

To Simon's horror, they were King's officers! One was General Pugh of the King's Dragoons. Simon had heard him described in the Dover prison as being a cruel, ruthless officer. With him was his aide-de-camp, a much younger man who was introduced as "my confidential officer—Mr. Philip Brackenbury."

There was no need for Simon to be introduced. He already appeared fast asleep.

As the coach swung along, General Pugh's voice came to Simon's ears. "Your Grace, I can't understand why you allow riff-raff as that young man plainly is, to travel in your coach."

"Charity knows no social barriers, my dear General," came the calm reply. "The man seemed ill and tired. I offered my help."

Philip Brackenbury spoke up. "General Pugh is right though, my lord. You take chances. This marsh country abounds at night with The Gentlemen."

"What are you talking about, Mr. Brackenbury?" the general asked gruffly. "You make no sense. What gentlemen?"

"That's what they call the smugglers in these parts, I understand, sir," his aide replied.

"Oh. *Those*," General Pugh grunted. "I know of them. But only as a pack of scoundrels. Gentlemen, indeed! *I'd* give them gentlemen! And I intend to. The ring will be smashed, and very soon." He patted the small case he carried on his lap. "I have my orders from the War Office and the Customs and Excise right here."

The archbishop sighed. "I don't envy you your task, General. From what I hear from my old friend, Dr. Syn, the whole countryside hereabouts protects them. Their friends are everywhere."

"Yes?" the general sneered. "Well I shall relish the task, my lord. Law enforcement has been too slack by far down here. Your friend, Dr. Syn, will see a change, I promise you."

Suddenly, the lumbering coach slowed, and the sound of the coachman's horn reached the passengers. The archbishop smiled. "Ah! Dymchurch ahead, I presume. This journey has taken less time than I—"

A loud cry from the outside was heard. "Halt there, in the King's name!"

"Whoa! Whoa!" And as the coachman brought the horses to a stop, the four passengers jolted back and forth in their seats. But this did not seem to interrupt the dreams of Simon Bates. He leaned back, eyes still closed as the coach door was flung open by a red-coated sergeant.

The sergeant leaned forward and swung his lantern into the coach. "We're looking for a . . . *Sir!*"

"What's this? Why are we stopping?" General Pugh demanded.

The sergeant nearly dropped the lantern in his hurry to give a smart salute.

"Well, what are you looking for, sergeant?" the general asked impatiently. "Speak up, man!"

"An escaped prisoner, sir, convicted for preaching treason."

"Treason!"

"Yes sir. He was to be hanged at Dover this morning. But he got away, sir."

"Hhmph!" General Pugh in that one snort, made it plain to all that no such thing could have happened had *he* been in charge of Dover prison —and he soon expected to be.

The archbishop leaned forward. "Treason, you say?"

"Yes, Your Grace. An American from the Colonies, so they say, sir."

There was a sudden silence. All eyes turned to the rumpled figure in the far corner. "You there!" the sergeant reached past Philip Brackenbury and swatted Simon's knee.

For a sleeping man, Simon Bates certainly seemed to wake up with his wits about him. In almost one motion, he grabbed the case from the general's lap and flung open the coach door.

"Stop that thief! After him!" General Pugh bellowed. He flung himself past Philip Brackenbury's boots and leaped through the open door. Brackenbury followed, and the sergeant and his men rushed around to the far side of the coach.

In the dark night, Simon ran blindly down the

road. Then as his eyes grew accustomed to the blackness, he cut over past rocks and bushes. But soldiers, mounted and on foot, were not far behind, swords drawn, and pistols at the ready.

Simon ducked into a dense clump of shrubbery. As heavy boots neared his hiding place, swords came thwacking down through the branches. Simon pressed closer to the earth. In his desperation, he hardly felt the slashing bite of the blade that struck his shoulder, and only huddled closer as the stomping footsteps moved on.

Then cautiously he peered out, spied a low stone wall, and made a run for it. Over he went, and plunged onward. In no time, he found himself squishing about in water-soaked ground. High reeds cut and slapped at his face and hands.

"He's over that way!" a voice rang out.

Simon stumbled forward—and straight to the edge of a pond. "It's my only chance," he gasped. "And may it be deep water!"

Silently as he could, he slid into the chilling pond. And none too soon! Philip Brackenbury, sword slashing, came through the reeds. Behind him came the sergeant. Simon took a deep breath. Lungs filled to bursting, he pushed off below the surface of the pond. He clung to rooted growth along the edge to keep from floating upward.

But try as he would, he had to release his breath. "They'll see the bubbles!" he thought despairingly. "This is the end!"

Using every ounce of will power he had, he

forced himself to make the rise to the surface slowly. As his head broke water, General Pugh's voice called out from the distance. "Any sign of him, Mr. Brackenbury?"

Then came the swishing sound of parting reeds and the splash of boots as Philip Brackenbury and the sergeant made their way back to the General. "No, sir!" the officer called out.

He turned to the sergeant. "The impertinent rogue! Sergeant, continue the search back along the road's edge. The General and I must be on our way."

"Sir!" the sergeant saluted, and trudged off.

Simon, chilled to the bone, not daring to splash his way out of the pond, remained where he was.

Dr. Syn, once again in the cozy warmth of the vicarage which was tucked like a chick beneath one wing of the village church, turned as Mipps walked into the study.

"Your records book, Doctor," he said, placing a large book on the desk.

Dr. Syn left the welcome blaze of the fireplace and seated himself at his desk. He glanced at the lettering on the book cover and smiled as he read the familiar title—*Register of Burials in the Parish of Dymchurch, County of Kent.*

Then picking up a quill pen, he turned to a marked page. "Ah, Sexton! This is splendid. I shall be able to enter a goodly list for this night's work. Sixty-eight kegs—no doubt King Louis' finest brandy, too. And nineteen bales of silk, not one yard of which but will be gladly paid for by the great ladies of England!"

As his pen scratched across the page, Mipps watched—and frowned.

"Now let us see," the vicar tickled his chin with the quill pen. "So much for Captain Delacroix's cargo. On Thursday it's the Dutchman's turn to make delivery. Oh, we *are* doing well, Sexton!"

Mipps hesitated. "Why do you go on taking these chances, Vicar? Heaven knows it is not making you rich. You take nothing. And as The Gentlemen don't know who their leader is, the parish can't thank you either."

Dr. Syn leaned back. "Well, Mipps, the fact remains that by smuggling luxuries they can now live, though however poorly. They can clothe themselves and their children, have a bit of food on the table, and still pay the taxes our King's Parliament has brought down on their heads. The Parliament! The people's representatives, mind you—treating those people as though they are dealing in cattle!"

The sexton shook his head. "You can't change that, Vicar. It seems to be the way of the world."

Dr. Syn's eyes flashed. "No, Mipps. Unjust laws can be changed as well as made. There's a new spirit in the world. Look at our American Colonies. Have we not heard rumblings from that far land? Rumblings of discontent! When men are taxed beyond bearing, they are robbed by their own government!" He shook his head. "The people must fight back as they can."

But Mipps stood his ground. "Men can't beat armies, sir."

Dr. Syn stood up. "Ideas can. Have you never really listened to the words you hear in Church, Mipps? *Faith can move mountains.* What we're doing here is no more than a pin prick against the side of a mountain. But thousands—nay, millions—put together—"

A quick, frantic rapping on the window cut short the vicar's words. A look of alarm spread over the sexton's face.

"See who it is," Dr. Syn ordered calmly. "Push back the drapes."

In the glow of the candlelit room, the pale, drawn face of Simon Bates appeared dimly on the other side of the diamond-shaped windowpanes.

It took some minutes to help the frozen, exhausted American into the study and settle him by the fireplace. And even longer for Simon Bates to tell his story.

He clutched a soaking wet case in his hands. "So after I got myself out of the pond, I hardly knew which way to go," he said tiredly. "I must have fainted, because the next thing I knew, I was lying on the ground, and an old woman was bending over me. She helped me to her cottage, and there she bound my injured shoulder. She was very kind. Mother Hathaway, she called herself."

Dr. Syn nodded. "We of Dymchurch know her well. She lives quite alone in her little cottage, and ekes out a scant living gathering and selling herbs. I understand why she sent you here. But tell me, young man—you are American, are you not?"

Simon nodded. "A foolish American, sir. I came to England to explain—to help make Englishmen understand what is happening in their Colonies. For my pains I was clapped into prison for preaching sedition!" He shook his head. "Imagine being branded a traitor and sentenced to hang for only trying to tell the truth to those who should know it."

He looked the vicar square in the eye. "I tell you this, sir, because Mother Hathaway told me I might find sanctuary here. But with troops still searching for me, I do not have the right to ask it and keep you ignorant of the reason why it is needed."

Mipps could keep silent no longer. "Sedition, Vicar!" he exploded. "That is a very serious charge."

Simon Bates spoke angrily. "We Colonials say that taxation without representation is unfair. We don't call that 'sedition' either."

Dr. Syn and Mipps exchanged quick glances. Then the vicar turned to Simon. "I can't deny you need sanctuary, Mr.—?"

"Bates. Simon Bates, sir."

Dr. Syn nodded. "Mr. Bates. But it would not be safe for either of us to hide you here."

"Then you'll give me up?"

"No." He arose. "Mipps, take Mr. Bates to Mrs. Waggett's inn. You'll know what to say. Mr. Bates, Mrs. Waggett will hide you until the coast is clear. But you must say *nothing*. Do not speak at all. Your American accent is plain, and we must not get Mrs. Waggett into trouble. The less she knows, the better for her."

Simon got to his feet. He held out the wet case. "I stole this in my escape from the coach. Will you take it, sir, and try to get it to one called 'The Scarecrow'?"

Dr. Syn frowned. "Why did you steal it?"

"I thought to find him myself. I heard about him while I was in the Dover prison. I had hoped to trade it to him for help in leaving England."

"From all I hear, Mr. Bates, I don't think you'd have found him. Many have tried and failed."

"Aye," Mipps added quickly. "He's like the devil, himself, so they say. Rides the marshes like a ghost. He comes and goes, nobody knows where!"

Dr. Syn led the way to the door. "I'll deal with it as I can, Mr. Bates. Meantime, you must go quickly."

Simon and Mipps followed the vicar. At the doorway Simon turned. "Whatever happens, sir, thank you, and God bless you."

No sooner had the two left than Dr. Syn hurried back to the case which he had left propped up by the fireplace.

Carefully, he opened it, removed the soaked papers, and carried them to the candlelight. One by one he separated and read each soggy sheet. When he came to the last one, he muttered aloud. "This *is* interesting! 'General Pugh,'" he read aloud. "'Dispatch of troops to Romney Marsh. Control the whole marsh area. Use whatever means necessary.'"

Dr. Syn dropped into his chair. "Well, well, WELL!"

CHAPTER 3

Philip Brackenbury heartily wished his commanding officer was off fighting the French instead of fighting with the father of the most beautiful girl Philip had ever met—Miss Kate Banks.

But knowing General Pugh's rough ways, Philip was very much afraid that Sir Thomas

Banks would never again invite the general—and his aide—to dine with his family at the Manor House. And Philip could not bear the thought of not meeting the lovely Kate many, many more times.

Dr. Syn, who was also a guest, could see a clash coming between the two older men. General Pugh's voice grew louder and Sir Thomas' face grew stonier.

The general waggled a finger almost under his host's nose. "I'm giving you fair warning, Sir Thomas. And if you're the justice of the peace in these parts, you'll want to see justice carried out —mine or any other. And it hasn't been up 'til now, eh? Hum?"

Sir Thomas' eyes sparked. "Are you telling me my duty, sir?"

General Pugh shrugged. "I'm a blunt man. I say what's in me mind." He strode back and forth. "You're the law here, and the law is being flouted. Revolutionaries and smugglers walking the roads! Wasn't I robbed last night not two miles from here? Right here in your district it was!"

He stopped pacing and glared at Dr. Syn. "In your parish, too, parson."

There was utter silence in the room. Kate Banks, pale as a snowflake, sat on the very edge of her brocaded chair. Standing beside her, Philip Brackenbury hoped *his* face wasn't matching the shade of his military redcoat.

General Pugh spun away from Dr. Syn. "Well, your silence makes it clear to me, sirs. You are quite satisfied with things as they are." His voice rose angrily. "Very well, then! You wait. You'll see *my* justice!"

Sir Thomas stiffened. "I don't care for your manner, sir. You are an officer. But a gentleman? It is said, 'a gentleman is one who never wittingly gives offense.' And what do you think of that, sir?"

General Pugh looked as though he wished he had a cannon ball handy. He glared briefly toward Philip Brackenbury. "Not having my commission bought for me by a gentlemanly father, but having made my own way in the army, I have my definition of a *soldier*." He again looked back at the others. "My definition of a good soldier," he repeated, "is one who achieves his aim and gets results. And the end justifies the means. Do I make myself clear, *gentlemen?*"

Kate Banks sprang to her feet, her dark eyes close to tears. "Father! General!" she begged.

A new voice spoke from the doorway. "And what means do you intend to use, sir?"

The general turned about. A slight, tall, and quite young lad stepped forward.

"My son, John, General," Sir Thomas managed to say calmly.

The general looked pleased. "I am happy that someone here is interested in His Majesty's plans for action in the marsh country. How'd'y do, young man. And to answer your question—. Every man has his price, and these smugglers will have theirs. And the price of freedom from the miseries His Majesty's government will bring down on their heads will be paid by *one* of these louts. He'll come forward and inform against this smuggling fellow. This—this 'Scarecrow,' as he calls himself. And I'll not use only my troops, either!"

Dr. Syn arose from his chair. "What then, General?" he asked politely. "I must warn you—I'm afraid you'll find the men in this parish are sturdy, independent folk. They—ah—they do not frighten easily."

General Pugh grinned. "And their women? They do not frighten easily, I suppose?"

"General!" Sir Thomas' voice rose in angry shock. "Women, sir! You would frighten women?"

General Pugh patted his gold braid and bowed slightly. "I'll do whatever I think fit to achieve my purpose here." His eyes snapped. "I think the women will talk soon enough when they start to lose their menfolk to the Navy. Ay, yes, Sir Thomas. I arranged it all before I left London. King George was only too pleased with my idea. The Navy needs sailors. Navy press-gangs will come to Dymchurch."

"Press-gangs!" Sir Thomas shook with rage.

"Father!" Kate implored.

"Keep out of this, Kate," her father ordered. He stepped nearly chin-to-chin with General Pugh. "Press-gangs! Do not dare to mention those blackguards in this house! In fact, sir, do not mention *anything* in this house. I've had all your talk I can stomach. Good day, sir."

Brushing past Kate and the others, Sir Thomas strode from the room.

General Pugh stared after him. "Well, what have I said wrong? I suppose you, Mr. Brackenbury, being the gentleman you are, can tell me. You look quite miserable. Speak up!"

John's eyes flashed. He saved the general's aide from having to reply. "My older brother, Harry, sir, was press-ganged into the Navy. He was clubbed insensible and dragged away to sea. That was four years ago. I was but eleven."

Tears were streaking down Kate's lovely face. "And Harry but eighteen," she cried. "It was his eighteenth birthday. We've not had a word from him nor about him, sir, in all those four years. Now you will understand my father's feelings, I'm sure."

Philip Brackenbury's hand touched Kate's arm gently. "I can, Miss Banks. Believe me."

General Pugh's jawline hardened. "The Navy needs men and must get them how it can. Do you deny that, Mr. Brackenbury?"

Philip flushed. "No sir."

"Then hold your tongue."

The general turned to John. "Please thank your father for his hospitality. If I upset him, I'm sorry. But I am under orders, and orders are given to be obeyed."

He bowed. "Mistress. Dr. Syn. Master Banks. Your men of the marshes have asked for rough treatment." He paused. "And rough treatment they shall get. Good day."

He strode to the door. Philip Brackenbury bent over Kate's hand. "Please, Miss Banks. Believe me when I express great regret," he murmured.

"Coming, Mr. Brackenbury?" the general snapped.

Hastily, Philip left the room.

"That dreadful man!" Kate choked.

Her young brother grinned. "You mean Mr. Brackenbury dreadful? Why, Kate! I thought him quite pleasant."

Rose-pink flowed into Kate's pale face. "How can you joke at such a time as this? You know my meaning. General Pugh's manner to Father was rude—and threatening, too!"

Dr. Syn looked calm as a pond. "Kate, my dear. We must have faith." He picked up his gloves. "I, too, must be away. The archbishop comes to tea with me this afternoon."

From the window Kate watched the vicar mount the fat, old pony, so familiar to all the villagers.

"Really, John," she frowned. "Sometimes I cannot help but think the vicar doesn't really care about what goes on in the world. He simply jogs about on his silly fat pony. That is—when he isn't drinking tea with archbishops!"

John chuckled. "Well, that's the life of a vicar, I suppose. What would you have him do? Join the smugglers?"

Kate suddenly giggled. "The vicar one of The Gentlemen of the Marshes? I can see him now, tearing through the night on old Fatty!"

But there were no giggles in the manor house that night. Here and there across the meadows, like giant bonfires, farm cottages burned and crackled as General Pugh's men put them to the torch!

CHAPTER 4

John and Kate Banks knew from the way their father marched into the breakfast room that General Pugh would shortly be facing a very angry village squire.

"I hope, Father," said Kate, "that you will not turn against Mr. Philip Brackenbury. After all, he cannot help being on that rude General Pugh's staff."

Her father made no reply. John, too, was silent. He hoped his father would not stir up the general's temper to the point that a curfew for all villagers would be imposed by the general in his determination to scare out the Scarecrow. "All I can do is to report to the vicar whatever is said between them," he thought.

Sir Thomas barely took time to say a good morning as he marched into the general's headquarters. He strode up to the general, seated behind a heavy desk. "I tell you, I will not tolerate your troops burning cottages on my land!"

General Pugh's eyebrows drew together. "Why not?" he asked coldly.

"Because the people here are my people. My family have been squires of Dymchurch for two hundred years."

"I must remind you, Sir Thomas—I act under the authority of His Majesty to maintain the law. As justice-of-the-peace, you are under that same law."

"Peace!" Sir Thomas exploded. "You've brought *war* here."

General Pugh waved his hand. "Nonsense! Offering a reward for the capture of this Scarecrow fellow who leads the rabble, was a peaceable method. It proved useless."

"Yes," Sir Thomas snapped back. "And so will be burning and terrorizing. My people will hate you. You'll be turning Englishman against Englishman. Further, sir, I will remind *you*—when your troops set fire to those cottages, they burned *my* property. I think King George will not wish the Crown held responsible for action such as that!"

For the first time, General Pugh hesitated. He leaned back in his chair. "Sir Thomas, I will make a bargain with you. We are both loyal subjects of his Majesty—only our methods of enforcing the law are different."

"Well?"

The general leaned forward. "As I take it, you do not approve of lawbreakers. True?"

Sir Thomas nodded.

"Then I suggest this—. You are the squire here. Who among your tenant farmers has been behind in his rents and then, quite suddenly, paid up?"

Sir Thomas looked thoughtful. "I see what you are getting at. You mean rentals may have been paid with smuggler's gold?"

"Exactly. Give me such names, and get the fellows to your house for questioning. Then leave the questioning to me. In fact, if this idea seems sensible to you, perhaps you might tolerate the presence of myself and my aide at the manor house for a short time. Your farmers will suspect nothing if you ask them to come there."

Sir Thomas tried not to show how little he looked forward to having General Pugh under his roof. It smacked of betraying his own people. "Yet what can I do?" he thought quickly. "This man could bring all Dymchurch down around our heads. And it is true that I must act on the side of His Majesty's law."

He nodded. "Agreed. There is one fellow that comes to mind now. You might make a start with him. He is a bad farmer. Pays little attention to his crops and his sheep. He is a widower with two sons and an old mother. I suspect he treats none of them too well. Ransley. That's the name. Joe Ransley."

"Very good. Have him at your house early tomorrow morning."

Sir Thomas turned to leave. "He'll be there, General. But one thing—*stop this burning*. I trust I have made my position clear."

General Pugh stood up and bowed. "Your servant, sir."

Kate and John didn't share the same feelings about the expected guests at the manor house. Kate was pleased that Philip Brackenbury would be returning. John was dismayed that General Pugh would be under their roof. "Can I get away nights now without my absence being noted?" he worried. "One thing I can do, though, is to try to hear what Joe Ransley will have to say tomorrow. At least, that's one thing that will be useful for the vicar to know."

So when the farmer arrived the next morning, John lingered by the door of the library.

"Good morning, Joe," the squire greeted

his tenant a bit uneasily. "General Pugh here, has asked to go over my account books and wishes to ask you a few questions."

General Pugh lost no time in being pleasant. "Joseph Ransley, North Farm, Bonnington Hills? You're not much of a farmer are you? Three years of bad harvests. Your sheep down to sixty head."

Joe twisted the cap in his hands. "It's poor land, sir. I do my best."

General Pugh stared at him coldly. "Yet you stay on it. I see from the squire's book that you were far behind in your rent. Suddenly you've paid it. How?"

"Yes, sir. I—well, I—."

Outside the door, it was plain to John that Joe Ransley was stumbling for an answer. After some mumbling, he heard Joe say, "I sold off some of my sheep, sir."

General Pugh peered at the account book. "Doesn't show that here."

"Well," Joe muttered, "the squire never questioned it."

"I do," the general snapped. "I don't think you have sold one of those sixty sheep. I think you're a smuggler and came by the money that way for your debts."

"Smuggler, sir?" Joe quavered. "I'm an honest man."

"Oh, are you now? Then prove it. Where are your bills of sale? Who did you sell to? What were the dates?"

"I don't keep records, sir," Joe replied sulkily.

The general stood up, walked around the desk and grabbed Joe's shirtsleeves. "Don't try lying to me, Ransley. You paid with smuggler's gold!" He gave Joe a rough shake. "Who's the man who leads you and pays you off? Answer me!"

"I don't know what you mean, sir," Joe stammered.

"Oh, yes you do! Maybe you'll understand this better—I'll give you a simple choice. I'll throw you in jail and I'll keep you there until questions are answered. Or—"

"*Jail!*" Joe exclaimed.

"Let me finish," the general roared. "Jail, yes. Unless you turn King's evidence and tell me all you know about that Scarecrow fellow and his smuggling gang!"

"I don't know nothing, sir. I swear I don't."

General Pugh didn't bother to say he didn't believe that. Instead, he gave Joe another shake. "You'll tell me where and when they meet. And you'll tell me where they go. Is that clear?"

Then suddenly his tone changed. "Nobody will know you talked, Ransley. Better think it over," he said almost pleasantly.

"But I don't know nothin', sir. I swear I don't."

"Very well." The general's voice turned rough again. "You're under arrest. Now. Mr. Brackenbury, seize this man."

"No, no! Wait, sir. Wait!"

"Well?"

"I said I don't know nothin' and I don't. But I might be able to find out. I'd try if you gave me a little time, sir."

"Forty-eight hours. No more!"

John's heart thudded. Ransley would betray them all! Once more, General Pugh's voice thundered in the library. "Remember! You'll either come forward with names of the men in this madman's gang—those so-called 'Gentlemen of the Marshes,' or you'll rot in jail. You've got forty-eight hours. Now get out!"

Hurriedly, John left his listening post, rushed from the house and ran as fast as he could around to the stables. "I've got to get to the vicar. Ransley is going to send us all to the gallows!"

Dr. Syn, as usual, listened as quietly as though John was telling him that the weather looked pleasant.

"One traitor's enough to get you hanged, sir," John said worriedly. "And the rest of us as well."

Dr. Syn merely reached for the teapot and refilled John's cup. "Mmm. And there's a shipment due from France tonight, too. With the general staying at the manor house, your head is really in the lion's mouth, isn't it?"

"You *will* let me ride with you tonight, won't you?" John asked.

Dr. Syn shook his head. "Much too risky, John. The General might suspect where you had gone."

"I don't see how!" John replied angrily—and not quite honestly.

Dr. Syn set down his cup. "You must obey orders as do the others, John. Your job is to keep your eyes on the good general."

He arose. "Well, there's work to be done between now and then. You must excuse me. And many thanks for the fine work you are doing, John."

A compliment from the vicar was to be treasured. Yet disappointment showed plainly on John's face as he mounted up and rode slowly home.

"I wonder how the vicar will ever manage *this!* What rotten luck!" he muttered.

In the vicarage, Dr. Syn talked with Mipps. "Ransley is one of our men. He has to be protected. Mipps, pack a food basket for old Mrs. Ransley. I shall ride out to Bonnington this afternoon. I'll find out what frame of mind Joe's in."

But as the vicar jogged up to the Ransley cottage, he no more than nodded to Joe who was pitching hay onto a cart. He went on to the cottage door where old Mrs. Ransley greeted him. Invited inside, he set the food basket on the table.

"Oh, Vicar!" the old lady exclaimed. "To come all this way to bring me something! You are so kind."

Dr. Syn patted her shoulder. "Joe and the boys looking after you properly?" he asked.

Mrs. Ransley's smile faded. "Joe's my stepson, Vicar. He looks out for nobody but himself. He cares for nobody else."

"Oh, surely that can't be true!"

Mrs. Ransley nodded. "It is. Whatever comforts we have, sir, me and the boys, is no thanks to him. No farming he does! It's because of—of—"

"Yes?" the vicar asked gently.

"You won't say I told?" Mrs. Ransley asked.

"I'm secret as the grave," the vicar replied. "You know that."

"It's because of the Scarecrow and his smugglers," the old lady whispered. "Joe's one of them. I know it."

"Surely he is not with that villain!" the vicar exclaimed in a shocked voice.

Mrs. Ransley shook her head. "The Scarecrow is no villain to us poor folk. Believe me, sir, if it were not for him, there's many hereabouts would starve. But Joe would betray the Scarecrow himself, if there was a penny in it for him." She lowered her voice even more. "I heard him talking to the boys. They're afraid of him, sir—his own sons afraid of him! He wants them to do something they don't want to do. But they'd do it, mind you! They're scared. Scared."

A voice spoke roughly from the doorway. "Time for your rest, isn't it? Get upstairs." Joe Ransley stepped into the cottage.

Mrs. Ransley paled and scuttled to the staircase.

"Yes, Joe. God bless you, Vicar." She started up the steps.

"Well, Vicar, it's me you wanted to see, I guess?" Joe asked.

"No. Just wished to say good day to you, Ransley. I brought a few things for your mother."

"*Step*mother," Joe said coldly. "Would you take a glass of cider before you leave?"

Dr. Syn smiled. "Thank you, but I must be going. By the way, Joe—speaking of cider. Somehow I am reminded of another drink. Brandy. I regret to say I've been hearing a great deal about its being smuggled to our shores under the leadership of the one called, 'Scarecrow'."

He watched Ransley sharply. "I'm surprised that among all the men in his gang, none have betrayed him as yet," he added.

Ransley shrugged. "Scared of him, they are, Vicar."

"Otherwise they would betray him?"

Ransley shook his head. "How would I know? But I don't aim to stay and find out—not with those troops a-burning and a-scaring. There's ways and means of getting away from this parish. And I've got plans."

There was the sound of a cart creaking up in front of the cottage. "I see your sons are driving up," the vicar said. "You have a busy day ahead, I'm sure. I'll be on my way."

But the vicar was in no great hurry after the cottage door closed behind him. He led his pony to the watering trough by the window. From inside, he heard Joe's son say, "We got another horse and cart, Dad, like you told us."

"Put it in the barn," Joe ordered. "Then, you, George, help Jim load all we can take on the cart. Drive up to the old oast house on Knoll Hill after sunset. I'll meet you there later with the Bonnington share of brandy kegs. We're taking 'em with us. Then we'll be gone!"

"Dad, what are you planning?"

"Mind your business."

"Will we take Grannie with us?"

"She'd be in the way. No. Now like I said—mind your own business and get to work."

Before the boys could "get to work," as their father had ordered, the vicar was up on old Fatty. He jogged down the lane. "The old oast house! Hmm. Now why didn't I think of that as a hideaway? That old oven up there hasn't roasted any hops since Sir Thomas built the new oast a good two years ago."

He chuckled. "Hops! Well, now that gives me an idea. I shall just see to it that Mr. Philip Brackenbury 'hops' up there this very evening. We must plan a surprise party for Joe Ransley. Can't have mutiny among Scarecrow's men!"

By the time he met Mipps at the vicarage, his idea was well thought out. Quickly, he outlined Ransley's plans. "We're going to make an example of Ransley, Sexton. It will teach the others a lesson they won't forget in a hurry. Betrayal among the Scarecrow's men is a worse danger than are General Pugh's troopers."

"Will you postpone tonight's run, Vicar?" asked Mipps.

"No, indeed. That cargo from France is too valuable for that."

"But if Ransley steals part of it, won't that make the Scarecrow look a fool to all the rest?"

The vicar smiled. "Mipps, as I said, we have to protect Ransley and yet teach him a lesson at the same time. Ride to the manor house and tell Master John to speak to Mr. Philip Brackenbury of a rumor going about. John might suggest that troops be at the Knoll Hill oast house tonight. And to hold Ransley's sons and await Joe's arrival. While Mr. Brackenbury is doing that, we'll be on the beach unloading the cargo."

Mipps looked puzzled. "I don't see, Vicar, how getting Ransley arrested by the King's troops is going to *protect* him. Or us, either. Then he'd be *sure* to tell all he knows."

Dr. Syn smiled cheerfully. "Never fear, Mipps. I have plans for Ransley, the kegs, and the King's troops as well! Now off with you! We've no time to lose."

While Mr. Philip Brackenbury and his troops watched and waited at the Knoll Hill oast house, the Scarecrow talked in a low voice with the Dutch captain.

"But I don't understand, Mynheer Scarecrow,"

the captain said. "Though of course I shall do as you say," he added hastily as he looked up into the glowering eyes behind the hideous mask.

The Scarecrow tossed him the usual money bag. "Full payment, and see that you follow my instructions *exactly*!" he demanded.

The bewildered captain shook his head as he watched the wild figure gallop up to the head of the line of carts and ponies. "It is true. The Englishman is as insane as the mask he wears!"

He turned to his crew and in a whisper repeated the Scarecrow's mad orders.

At the other end of the cove, Scarecrow was on to other important business. "Scannel, Davis— this is the Romney village share. Take the marsh road eastward. Hurry!"

He turned to another member of The Gentlemen. "Sam, this load is for Dymchurch. Go!"

Last, came Ransley. "Ah! Now what remains for you? Take your cart back along the beach. The last kegs are for Bonnington. On your way, man!"

CHAPTER 5

All Dymchurch was buzzing with the news the King's soldiers had caught Joe Ransley smuggling. He would face trial as soon as a special prosecutor had arrived from London. There hadn't been such excitement since last winter when a storm threatened to break the dykes and let thundering seas sweep over the low-lying Romney Marsh just outside the village.

On the morning of the trial, even Mrs. Waggett had closed the inn doors so that she would not miss the performance of Mr. Fragg, the King's Prosecutor, who had come into town the night before.

Indeed, except for that silent stranger, the American hidden in Mrs. Waggett's attic, there was scarce a soul in Dymchurch-below-the-Wall who was either not seated in the jammed courtroom, or milling about the entrance, awaiting the outcome of the trial.

Those inside watched Prosecutor Fragg go up to the judge's bench where Sir Thomas sat.

"The court has heard the evidence of these wretched men," he said loudly, and waved a hand toward Joe and his two sons. "They were caught red-handed with twenty kegs of contraband brandy in their possession. Cheating his Majesty's revenue is exactly what they were doing. They have no defense."

The prosecutor glared around the courtroom before turning back to Sir Thomas. "I demand that an example be made of them to all smugglers and to their infamous leader. I demand they suffer the full penalty of the law."

Then Fragg stepped to the side of General Pugh. "Unless, of course, as I am instructed by General Pugh, that they here and now confide the name of their leader called 'Scarecrow'."

He paused. "In which case, the Crown will not press for their death by hanging."

In the stand, Ransley burst forth. "But I don't *know*, sir. I tell you—nobody knows."

Fragg marched to him and leaned close. "But you've *seen* him. You've *spoken* to him."

"Only to get orders," Ransley gasped.

"And where did he hold these meetings? You *can* tell me that, I suppose."

"Different places, sir. On the beach. On the marsh. In somebody's barn."

"Whose barn?" the prosecutor snapped, "Tell the court."

There was a dead silence in the courtroom. "Whose barn?" Prosecutor Fragg thundered.

"Somebody's. That's all." Ransley quavered.

"*Tell the court!*" Fragg blazed.

Ransley's voice dropped to a croak. "I don't want to swing for the likes of *him!*"

There was an instant buzz and hum of voices in the jammed courtroom, and at the same time, Dr. Syn entered at the back of the long aisle.

Sir Thomas pounded his gavel. "Silence!" he demanded.

Dr. Syn came striding forward, waving a paper in his hand. "By your leave, Your Worship!"

"Yes, Dr. Syn You may speak," said Sir Thomas.

"I—I've just come from my home where I found this note. It is a threat, sir, and I do not care for threats." He handed the paper to Sir Thomas.

"What's this!" the astonished Sir Thomas exclaimed. He read aloud to the courtroom. " 'If the Reverend Dr. Syn speaks for the prisoners on trial, he will answer to the Scarecrow with his own life.' "

There was an uproar in the room. Sir Thomas pounded for silence. General Pugh rose to his feet. "Who would want to threaten you, Parson? Were you about to speak for these scoundrels? And, if so, who would know that?"

Dr. Syn looked a little foolish. "Well, General, word does get spread around, I know. And—well, I just happened to mention to my sexton, Mipps, a point of law I'd thought of regarding this case. I should have recalled that Mipps *does* spend some free time talking at Mrs. Waggett's inn."

There was a ripple of laughter in the crowd.

"What point of law did you mention, Vicar?" Sir Thomas asked sharply.

"Well, one which, if you will allow me, would certainly save these unhappy prisoners from punishment, were it to be proved true."

Prosecutor Fragg sprang up. "I object, Your Worship. The Crown demands—"

"*If* you please, Mr. Fragg," Sir Thomas snapped. "Continue, Vicar. What is this point of law?"

Dr. Syn nodded. "Thank you. Well, Your Worship, that note gave me reason to suppose the Ransleys walked into a trap. I wondered—. Would this arch smuggler waste twenty kegs of costly spirits to bait his trap at the old oast house? I still wonder about that. Have the contents of the kegs been examined?"

There was a pause. General Pugh, Prosecutor Fragg, Mr. Philip Brackenbury, and Sir Thomas, glanced at each other.

Dr. Syn went on. "If—if indeed they contained contraband, then of course the prisoners must stand condemned. But—ah—should not the kegs be examined before sentence is given?"

Sir Thomas nodded. "Has counsel for the Crown any objection to this?"

"No. No, of course not," Prosecutor Fragg answered smugly.

After Sir Thomas gave the order that the kegs be opened, Dr. Syn turned to General Pugh. "I trust I can rely on the protection of your troops in the matter of my safety?"

"Of course," the general replied.

The court and onlookers had not long to wait for the beadle, officer of the court, to return.

He held out a cup to Sir Thomas. "Your Worship, each keg has been opened. Each contains this—sea water."

"SEA WATER!" General Pugh, his aide, and Prosecutor Fragg burst out.

Dr. Syn bowed. "Surely there is no law in England that condemns a man carrying kegs of water."

Only six people in the courtroom failed to burst into wild laughter—the King's officers, the Prosecutor, and the three Ransleys.

Sir Thomas finally remembered the dignity of his office. He rapped his gavel. "Case dismissed. The prisoners Ransley, can go free."

In the loud confusion, General Pugh turned on Fragg. "You incompetent bungler!" he raged. Then he spun around to face his aide. "You fool!" he charged angrily. "I thought you were a fool, Mr. Brackenbury, and now I know it! Taking action into your own hands! Not consulting me! Get out of my sight! Now!"

"Yes, sir," Philip answered stiffly. But already the general had shouldered him aside and was stomping angrily from the courtroom.

Joe Ransley moved from the guards to Dr. Syn. "Thank you, Vicar, for what you have done."

Dr. Syn looked stern. "You escaped the law, Ransley, but I fear your Scarecrow leader won't let you escape *him*. Nor will any of his men who now know you as a traitor. You'd best get away as far as you can from this parish."

Ransley turned and promptly bumped into General Pugh. "You've got off *this* hook," the general bit out, "but you're still on mine, Ransley. Remember that!"

Dr. Syn left the courtroom with Mipps and John. "John, I want you to keep an eye on Ransley from sunset on. Mipps, you watch Mr. Fragg —now."

"And what do you plan to do now, sir?" John asked.

The vicar smiled. "Think, my good lad. Think."

Sir Thomas was the only pleased person around his dinner table that evening. General Pugh was not talking to his aide. His aide was trying to pretend all was well. Kate was realizing that her dear Philip was being blamed for not testing the contents of the kegs. But Sir Thomas was just glad that the day's events were over and wanted to forget them as soon as possible!

He would have not been so happy had he known that John, absent from the table, was standing guard at the Ransley farm.

"Young men will be young men," he chuckled as he carved the beef. "John is no doubt out playing with his friends."

Meanwhile at Mrs. Waggett's inn, another conversation was taking place between Mr. Mipps, the sexton, and Mr. Fragg, the King's Prosecutor.

"This case you came down for from London must have been a great disappointment to you, sir," Mipps said to the man at his elbow.

Fragg eyed him coldly. "And who might you be?" he asked.

"Me, sir? Mr. Mipps, sir. Sexton, verger, carpenter, and undertaker. I'm what is known as a right-hand man to the vicar, Dr. Syn."

"Indeed?" Mr. Fragg's voice lost none of its coolness. "You seem to mind all sorts of business but your own."

Instead of becoming angry, Mipps chuckled. "Oh, that *is* good, sir. Very good! You are indeed witty, sir. I *do* seem to mind a great many things!"

Fragg did not bother to reply, but edged away from Mipps.

Not at all bothered, Mipps edged right along. "If you want to know anything about anyone in these parts, sir, I'm the man for you, sir. You see," he said softly, "in these parts, I'm the man to come to. Being a servant of the Church, I'm the soul of quiet action, sir. And on the side of the law, too. I thought the general's words to you—which I just happened to overhear—were most unkind!"

"Mmm," Fragg murmured but this time glanced quickly at Mipps.

"Well, I suppose, Mr. Fragg, you'll be on your way back to London tomorrow, now that your business here is over."

Mr. Fragg turned to face Mipps. "Perhaps it is not," he replied. "You say you are on the side of the law?"

"Naturally."

"Then you realize the law was blocked today, don't you?"

"Ah!" Mipps sighed. "That wicked Ransley! To think he'd fill kegs with sea water! The villain! I never guessed him to be so clever."

General Pugh's charge of "incompetent fool," still rang in Mr. Fragg's ears. He thought a moment. "How far away does this Ransley live, Sexton?"

"Oh, I'd say about a good hour's ride from here on a good horse, sir."

Fragg twiddled his fingers about. "Can you get me a good horse without all the world knowing tonight?"

Mipps managed to look surprised. "Tonight? Why tonight, sir?"

Fragg scowled. "I asked a simple question. Can you?"

Mipps nodded. "Yes. Yes I can. But—ah—mum's the word, eh, Mr. Fragg?" He winked.

Fragg winked back.

"Then I'll meet you at the fork in the sea road. Half an hour it will be. I'll have a horse for you there."

He stood up, bowed to Mrs. Waggett and to his many friends. "Goodnight, lads. It's off I am to my well-earned rest."

Everyone waved him a cheerful goodnight.

In his hiding place at the corner of Joe Ransley's barn, time was passing slowly for John Banks. Shortly after dark, old Grannie Ransley had been boosted to the top of a heavily laden farm cart. There seemed to be scarcely room for her small figure, and certainly no room for George and Jim. On foot, the two led the old horse down the lane.

John wished Dr. Syn could have seen them. The boys had told no names in court, and John was sure that the kindly pastor would have helped them to make a fresh start in a new place.

"I wonder—why didn't Joe Ransley go, too?"

John asked himself. "He must know the Scarecrow will not let him off as easily as he was let off in court today. Maybe Joe has something else up his sleeve! The vicar must have some reason to think that Joe would stay behind."

The distant sound of hoofbeats reached his ears. "One horse," he thought. "Whose?"

The lone horseman dismounted at the cottage and pounded hard on the door. When it opened, John caught one quick glimpse of Joe Ransley's visitor—none other than the Crown's prosecutor, Lawyer Fragg.

"What do you want with me?" he heard Ransley ask.

"To talk with you," came the reply.

The door closed behind the lawyer, and John began to move quietly toward the cottage.

"Master John," a low voice called out softly. "Wait. It's Mipps, sir."

Almost out of breath, Mipps stepped out of the shadows. "Left my horse back by the tree where I saw yours tied. Has Fragg gone into the cottage?"

"Yes. How'd you know he was coming here?"

Mipps grinned. "I got him the horse he rode. Then I followed. Where can we hear what's going on?"

"Let's try around at the back."

There was no trouble in hearing or seeing what was going on inside the cottage. A back window stood open and there was a full view of Fragg and Ransley.

"We're alone?" asked Fragg.

Ransley nodded. "The vicar. He came. Gave the old lady money, he did. And told the boys that the three of them should go. Said General Pugh wouldn't be after *them!*"

"Then why did they leave?" Fragg asked sharply.

"The vicar said as how they should have a new start," Joe answered gloomily. "I'm getting out of here, too, soon's I can."

Fragg laughed. "*You!* Where'd you run to? This Scarecrow fellow, or his followers, will stop you." He clicked his fingers. "Your life isn't worth *that* unless I help you—which I won't do without *you* helping *me*."

Ransley looked angry. "You can't touch me now. You can't try me in court twice for the same reason."

Fragg laughed again. "Don't worry. You won't be in court again. You got off because of a trick. But don't tell me *you* put that seawater in those kegs! The Scarecrow was onto you, and he'll make sure that General Pugh won't get those names out of you!"

Joe jumped to his feet. "Run from the Scarecrow! Run from the general!" He rubbed his aching forehead.

Fragg grinned. "Stop rubbing your head! You tell me something I want to know, and I'll give you something to run *with*—and the general won't be after you, either."

Joe's eyes narrowed. "What are you talking about?"

"The reward money, you fool! Bring me your list of names at this time tomorrow night. Twenty names will be enough. I'll meet you at this same time at the old castle ruins. Meet me, and you shall have nine hundred and ninety-nine more coins like this!" He flung a gleaming gold coin on the table.

Joe stared.

"You'll be safe from General Pugh because you'll have done your duty. You'll be safe from the Scarecrow because the Department of Revenue will protect you. And you'll have money!"

"And nobody will know?" Joe asked slowly.

"Nobody." Fragg turned to the door. "Tomorrow night, then, *at the castle ruins*. Fail me and you are finished."

Inside the cottage, Joe Ransley stared at the circle of gold.

Outside, Fragg mounted his borrowed steed. He chuckled. "I'm sure General Pugh would like to be the hero of this occasion tomorrow night. I'll go now and invite him to be present—but *at the old monastery!* Then we'll see who looks an 'incompetent fool'!"

CHAPTER 6

Sir Thomas' servant opened the library door. "Mr. Fragg to see General Pugh, sir."

"Show him in," the general growled.

Mr. Fragg came in, his face almost beaming. For a defeated prosecutor who had looked ridiculous in court only that afternoon, he seemed strangely happy.

"Good evening, General," he said, smiling broadly.

"Ah, Mr. Prosecutor," the general spoke coldly. "What do you want at such an hour as this? I would have guessed you were well on your way to London by now."

Fragg's smile grew even broader. "I'll leave when my business here is finished," he said smoothly. "I believe you called me an 'incompetent' today."

"So?"

Fragg's eyes blazed. "*So* I've come to tell you that I'll make you eat those words."

General Pugh laughed heartily. "You have, have you? And how will you make me do that?"

"By bringing to justice, here in Dymchurch, enough of that smuggler's gang to smash the ring. And more than likely, catch him, too, in the bargain."

General Pugh leaned back and eyed Fragg coldly. "Well, well, well. Just like that, eh? And when will this big haul of yours take place, if I may ask?"

"This time tomorrow night," Fragg snapped. "Of course, you'll want your troops to be there, General."

"Oh?"

"You'll surely wish to supply me an armed escort when *I* go to round up these criminals. I don't imagine they'll come along without a struggle, General."

General Pugh stood up. He looked closely at the King's prosecutor. "First sensible thing you've said. I don't imagine they will." He hesitated. "And where is this event to take place?"

"At the old monastery," Fragg replied.

"I'll head the troops myself," General Pugh said.

Mr. Fragg's eyes gleamed. "Very good of you, sir. Now I shall say goodnight. Until I have your apology, we really have nothing else to say. Do we?"

"Nothing at all, Mr. Fragg."

As Mr. Fragg started toward the door, the general called out. "Mr. Fragg. I believe I do have one more thing to say—I hope this time you've not bitten off more than you can chew."

Mr. Fragg's eyes blazed again. But he bowed. "It's a good thing there are more brains in my profession than the evidence would seem to show is in yours. Goodnight, again, to you, General."

Dr. Syn looked from John to Mipps. "So Fragg acted after all," he said frowning. "I'd hoped he'd taken the Royal Mail coach to London after the disgrace of the trial. And I'd hoped that fear would keep Ransley silenced. But he will sell us all, you can be sure of that."

"We should get rid of him, sir," Mipps urged. "There'd be plenty willing to do it—them he's planning to hand over to the Law."

Dr. Syn shook his head. "I'll not have murder,

Mipps," he said shortly. "The Gentlemen of the Marsh take the King's revenue. Yes. But a man's life? No!"

John looked doubtful. "How is this matter to be solved, Vicar? We're no murderers, but—." He flung his hand out helplessly.

Dr. Syn walked to his desk and sat down. "I do believe a plan has come into my head that might solve our problem. If so, it would teach a lesson to all would-be traitors, and a lesson to King George's revenue men who offer blood money for lives!"

"What are we to do, sir?" Mipps said.

Dr. Syn smiled. "Tomorrow you must rise early, Sexton. Your job will be to build a coffin."

John gasped. "A *coffin!* But I thought, sir—"

"And John," Dr. Syn went on, "your task is to get word to The Gentlemen. We meet at Broken Barn tomorrow night."

To Mr. Fragg, riding along in the moonlight, it seemed that the old castle ruins stood out against the sky as still as death.

He looked around nervously, dismounted, and tied his horse to a scraggly tree. Slowly, he stepped toward the old stone walls, and then on to the darkness within.

"Ransley?" he called. His voice sounded strange and hollow to him.

"Answer him, Ransley!" The hoarse words sounded loudly almost in Fragg's ear. "Step forward. Show him how the Scarecrow deals with traitors!"

Fragg whirled back toward the entrance. Too late! Several "gentlemen" pinned his arms to his side. And as he was shoved out into the moonlight, a gag was pushed into his mouth.

Then, dragged out beside him, came Joe Ransley.

The Scarecrow laughed hideously. "Now, my merry men, behold the two who would betray us! Take them to their just punishment!"

Bound, gagged, and blindfolded, Ransley and Fragg were hauled off by masked men to Broken Barn.

At the monastery, a quite different scene was taking place. Excepting for the dull *clumps* of pawing horses, there was ordered quiet among the general's troopers.

General Pugh, by now chilled to the bone by the damp marsh night, began to wonder if he had misunderstood Fragg's instructions. "I'm sure he said 'old monastery'—but could it have been 'old castle ruins'? Each is a landmark in these parts." He sneezed loudly, and his horse shied.

Behind him, a trooper sneezed. "Silence that man!" the general snapped. "No sneezing—and that's an order."

He sneezed again. "Well, there is nothing to do but wait and catch my death from cold!" he exclaimed angrily to himself.

At Broken Barn, Ransley and Fragg were securely tied to chairs. Ransley's blindfold was removed. A frightening sight met his eyes. Dim lantern light showed that he and Fragg were surrounded by masked men, standing motionless, silent, and—menacing.

Worst of all to Ransley, was the sight of the dread Scarecrow standing before him!

"Remove the prisoner's gag," the hoarse voice thundered.

"Why'd you bring me here?" Ransley cried out. "I'm one of you, ain't I?"

"No, Ransley," the Scarecrow answered in a deadly voice.

He sat down at a table. "This court is now in session. Remove the other prisoner's gag and uncover his eyes so that he may see the Scarecrow's Justice."

Fragg, blindfold removed, stared wildly at the scene around him. He pulled at his bonds. "You pack of scoundrels!" He screamed. "In the King's name, I demand that you release me."

"Gag him again," the Scarecrow ordered. "Now —we begin.

"Joe Ransley, you stand charged with treachery. How say you? Guilty or not guilty?"

"I ain't hurt you none, Scarecrow," Joe muttered.

"Guilty or not guilty?"

"Not guilty."

The Scarecrow beat his fist on the table. "First witness called. Curlew!"

John Banks, wearing his Curlew disguise, stepped forward with a sheet of paper. He handed it to the mad figure before him.

Scarecrow read it aloud. "This is a sworn statement of events witnessed last night," he concluded. It told of the conversation that John had overheard. "Now, second witness. Hellspite," he called, putting down Curlew's paper.

Hellspite, otherwise sexton of Dymchurch, handed over his sworn statement. It, too, was read aloud.

The Scarecrow arose. "And now my statement, Gentlemen."

He turned to Ransley. "On the last run of my Gentlemen, you attempted to steal from us. You were caught and put on trial by His Majesty's Government."

"I didn't hurt you none," Joe Ransley burst out. "And I was let off in court, too."

Scarecrow held up his hand. "Only because of a parson's help. And I'll deal with *him* later. You told the prosecutor at your trial, that you'd betray me. You said, *'I won't swing for the likes of him.'* In spite of the oath you made with me—*the oath every man here has taken*—you said those words."

Scarecrow paused. "What kind of man will sell his friends to the hangman for gold, Ransley?"

"I ain't done that."

"And never intended to?" Scarecrow asked sternly.

"No."

Scarecrow sat down. "Empty his pockets," he ordered.

Curlew and Hellspite stepped forward. Then Curlew carried a piece of paper to the table and one golden coin.

"Ah! Here are the names he would sell. Perhaps your names, Gentlemen, are among them. And here is the gold coin sworn to in the statements we have heard. You were taking this list of names to Fragg tonight!"

Ransley yelled out. "All right! I was! So I was! You was after me. The Army was after me."

Scarecrow's voice rolled to the very rafters. "You stand convicted by your own words! You are a cheat, liar, traitor! Gentlemen of the jury, how say you? Is the prisoner guilty or not guilty?"

Cries lifted to the gloom of the roof above. "Guilty! Guilty!"

Scarecrow raised his arm and silenced the smugglers. "Guilty it is. And, Joe Ransley, this court sentences you thus." He pointed to a noose dangling from the blackness of the rafters.

"No! *No!*" Ransley shouted.

"Cover the lanterns, Curlew. Gag the prisoner. Spare us the sight and sound of this coward's hanging."

In the dark, Scarecrow pulled on the rope. Chair

and all, Joe Ransley was lifted into the overhead blackness.

"Lanterns!" Scarecrow cried.

All eyes looked upward, including Fragg's. In the gloom above, only a dim outline of chair legs could be seen dangling in the near-darkness.

"Very well," Scarecrow spoke loudly and quickly. "Justice is done. So ends all men who would betray the Scarecrow and The Gentlemen of the Marshes."

Fragg's face was white. "My turn is next," he muttered.

"Now, the next prisoner. Fragg. Fragg, give my Gentlemen the King's gold—the rest of the reward money you promised the villain, Ransley."

Curlew took the money bag from Fragg and dumped it onto the table.

"Share it among you, Gentlemen." Scarecrow flung his frightful cloak back. "And remember the Scarecrow's justice!"

He turned to Fragg. "As for you—my Gentlemen will escort you a goodly distance, *blindfolded*. And then, Fragg, GO. Never return to these parts if you value your life."

The moment the last smuggler of the "jury" had left Broken Barn, Scarecrow, Curlew, and Hellspite worked the rigging that held Joe Ransley's chair high aloft. But Ransley was not dead! The hangman's rope was cleverly knotted around the

back of the chair. The noose had never been pulled tight around his neck.

As the chair was lowered to the barn floor, Scarecrow stared down at Joe Ransley. "You just fainted, Ransley, you are not dead. But to all the men of the marshes you have been executed. General Pugh will learn of this 'death.' The Army will now learn you are dead. So—I give you one hour to leave Dymchurch, Bonnington Hills, Romney Marsh and Kent—*forever*. Get away from here or otherwise you'll *really* die."

He loosened Joe Ransley's bonds. "Run for your life, Ransley."

And once again, the dread laugh Joe Ransley had heard ring out over the marshes, lifted and echoed in the silent barn.

"RUN FOR YOUR LIFE!"

Next morning, the London-Dover Royal mail coach slowed to allow a funeral procession to pass by.

Prosecutor Fragg peered through the window just in time to see the coffin carried by four men. On it was lettered,

HERE LIES JOSEPH RANSLEY
DEPARTED THIS WORLD AS THE RESULT
OF AN ACCIDENT
- 1775 -

He shuddered and rapped on the window glass. "Drive on!" he shouted to the coachman.

Dr. Syn glanced after the coach and then looked quickly at his sexton. Mipps spoke solemnly. " 'So end all traitors!' And the Scarecrow's men still ride the marshes!"

"Can *nobody* stop the villain?" the vicar asked, a twinkle in his eye.

"They'll try sir," Mipps replied. "Look who rides toward us now."

General Pugh, at the head of the troopers, brought his horse to a standstill. He glanced down at the coffin and then toward Dr. Syn.

"Save some space in your graveyard, parson, for the Scarecrow. Because I swear to you he'll be there—and soon!"

With that, he gave a mighty sneeze.

Dr. Syn bowed. "Good luck to you, General. And do take care of that cold you have."

"Forward!" Pugh roared.

The troopers rode on.

"They seem to be heading for Dover, wouldn't you say sir?" asked Mipps.

"I'd say so," the vicar smiled. "Wouldn't it be pleasant if General Pugh took a notion to keep right on going to London?"

Mipps sighed. "Little chance of that, I'd venture to say, Vicar."

But the sexton was wrong. London was exactly where the general was going—and he was not looking forward to the visit. His monarch, King George III, had commanded his presence in London for a personal report on his general's lack of success in putting down smuggling along His Majesty's south coast.

General Pugh, as he rode along, felt there was little to choose between the Dymchurch graveyard and the Royal Palace!

CHAPTER 7

Philip Brackenbury had smarted under General Pugh's parting words. "I leave you in charge of headquarters, Mr. Brackenbury. I wish I could say, 'in command.' But your past blunders force me to tell you that you will take no independent action while I am gone."

But Philip soon learned there was a brighter side to life. Kate's opinion of him was as high as the general's was low. And now on the first evening of the general's return, Philip could hardly bear knowing that both were invited to dine at the manor house.

"Perhaps the army life is not for me," he thought, looking across the table at the general. "I love my country, but there must be another way to serve it than under the thumb of General Pugh!"

After dinner, he and Kate wandered to a sofa. Across the room, Sir Thomas and Dr. Syn played a game of chess under the watchful eye of the general—and with much advice based on the general's knowledge of military tactics.

"Hang it all, Vicar!" Sir Thomas exclaimed, as he lost the game. "You'd think I could beat you once in a while." He looked up at the general. "Our vicar is clever as a fox!"

"Would you care to play, general?" Dr. Syn asked.

The general frowned. "No. I have no patience for idle games," he said haughtily. "Even with a clever fox."

Young John strolled in just then. "But you *hunt* a fox, don't you, sir?"

Before the general could reply, a servant stepped into the room. "Sir Thomas, a messenger has arrived who wishes to see the general."

"Show him in," General Pugh ordered, not giving his host the chance to reply.

So all were present when a sergeant entered with

news—the sort of news Sir Thomas could hardly bear having mentioned in his house.

"General Pugh, sir," the sergeant saluted.

"Well?"

"We have a squadron searching the marshes and cooperating with the Naval picket."

"I knew that," the general snapped.

"All the press-gang men who jumped ship at Dover have been recaptured but one."

"But *one!* What do you mean, sergeant? How was he allowed to escape?"

"He was seen heading for Dymchurch an hour ago. But we lost him. Permission asked to carry out a house to house search, sir?"

"Certainly!" General Pugh roared. "And thoroughly! Spare no one!"

The sergeant saluted and departed. General Pugh turned excitedly to Sir Thomas. "This is the chance I've been waiting for! To turn this village inside out! I don't wonder a deserter would head this way. Your people here are a lawless lot, Sir Thomas. They shield the Scarecrow, don't they? And his band of smugglers? Why would they hesitate to flout the law further and take on a Naval deserter?"

"You've no proof of that, general," Dr. Syn said quietly.

General Pugh snorted. "*Proof!* They'd do it. That's all I need to say. And if I find *one* of them, *any* of them, there'll be some hanging here!"

For a moment, not a word was said. Then Dr.

Syn arose. "Thank you for a delightful dinner and evening, Sir Thomas. Kate." He bowed. "Time I was getting home."

"I'll see you to the gate, Vicar," John said.

Goodnights were exchanged, and the two left the room. But as John was helping the vicar with his cloak, General Pugh's voice carried loudly and angrily to the hallway.

"Sir Thomas, the marshes are now under military law. I have my authority from the King. If you have any objection, complain to His Majesty. Now, sir, recalling your feelings about press-gangs, I shall not press my society upon you longer. Goodnight to you, sir. Mr. Brackenbury! We are leaving."

Dr. Syn murmured, "We'll be having the military's company a little longer than I'd wish."

"I should be on my way now to warn Mrs. Waggett the inn will be searched," John said worriedly.

But as the two officers left the drawing room, Kate sped up to General Pugh. Shyly, she placed her hand on his sleeve. "General, won't you allow Mr. Brackenbury to stay a little longer? Just as a favor to me? Please!"

General Pugh shrugged. "A very little longer. Mr. Brackenbury, I shall be waiting outside for you. And I shall expect you *soon*." He picked up his hat, and John held out his military cape.

Nobody but Kate was pleased by this sudden turn of events. As the three went out the door she looked up at Philip. "Speak to Father now, Philip."

"All right, Kate," he sighed. "But I fear his opinion of the Army is not going to help us." He pressed her hand.

"Oh, I'm sure it's only the general who upsets Father so! It's all that raving!"

Outside, Hobbs, Sir Thomas's groom, waited by the horses. He touched his cap as Master John and the guests came out. "Beggin' pardon, young sir," he said, "but we've stabled the vicar's pony. Noted he'd cast a shoe. Shall I saddle up another mount?"

"Goodness me!" the vicar exclaimed. "Not one of Sir Thomas's spirited horses! I doubt I could stay in the saddle!"

The groom bobbed his head in sympathy. "Used to old Fatty you are, Vicar. Perhaps the pony cart then, Master John?"

John was about to agree when he felt Dr. Syn's elbow poke into his ribs. "That would be splendid as a choice, John," said Dr. Syn. "But why don't you send Hobbs off to bed? We'll see off the general and Mr. Brackenbury, and surely between us we can hitch up a pony cart."

Why didn't the vicar want Hobbs to bring the pony cart out to them? John wondered. But the vicar usually had good reasons for every action.

As Hobbs left for the servant's quarters, the general shook his head. "Vicar, you set a bad example for Master Banks. It is easy to see you had no Army training. There you would have learned to *command*—have others do your bidding."

The vicar nodded. "No doubt. John, you must remember that advice."

"Further," General Pugh said. "Had you been in the Army you would have learned by this time in life, how to ride a horse. And if you ask me, Vicar, 'Fatty' is a very unsuitable name for a pony ridden by a gentleman in a position of dignity."

The vicar sighed and was just about to reply when the general suddenly turned his gaze to the manor house. "Where is that fool Brackenbury?" he exclaimed impatiently. "Help me mount up, Master Banks," he demanded. "I'm leaving at once! I shall deal with Mr. Brackenbury later."

"Poor Philip," John said, as the general galloped off down the drive. "He's always getting dealt with later. Have you noticed?"

But the vicar seized John's elbow. "Quick, John. Don't worry about Philip. Worry about Harry."

"*Harry*!"

The vicar strode along as fast as he could toward the stables, John at his side. "Hasn't it crossed your mind, John, that Harry might be the deserter they're looking for?"

John turned pale. "But I don't understand, then, vicar. Why have we wasted time by having Hobbs sent off? And why not have accepted a fast horse? I thought it was the American who was on your mind."

"I prefer that the general believes I cannot ride well," Dr. Syn replied. "Further, if the deserter *is*

Harry, he might very well be hiding in the stables. I wished to have Hobbs nowhere near."

At the stable door, John took down a lantern and lighted it. The vicar began to open the door —and then stopped. His eyes had glimpsed a tall figure, knife glinting in the lantern light quickly step behind it.

"If you're the deserter," Dr. Syn whispered rapidly, "we're here to help, not harm you. I'm Dr. Syn, vicar of Dymchurch."

A weak voice exclaimed, "Dr. *Syn!*" The door fell open.

John raised the lantern. Dr. Syn gasped. "It *is* Harry! Your brother, Harry, John!" He took a step toward the gaunt, hollow-cheeked man. "My lad! What have they done to you?"

John stared unbelievingly. "We—we thought you dead!"

Harry tried to smile. "And you are *John!* I can't believe the child I remember is this tall fellow! You were not much more—"

Dr. Syn stopped him. "Harry, no time for talk. Quick! Tell me—have you just come?"

Harry nodded. "But I saw soldiers through the window."

"They search for you," Dr. Syn said gravely. "They hang deserters from the Navy. Harry, we must hide you at once. Every house in Dymchurch is to be turned upside down to find you. We must make haste."

"But, Vicar!" John gasped. "Father. We must

think of Father. He's longed all these years for one glimpse of Harry."

Dr. Syn's hand fell gently on John's arm. "Steady, lad. We'll get Harry out of here by pony cart. I'll hitch up while you go to the house and bring out Sir Thomas. But do *not* tell him Harry is here. His shock and alarm might be observed by the household. Make up any excuse. Hurry!"

Philip had been right when he'd told Kate that her father disliked the Army. Sir Thomas, his mind on press-gangs, military law, and all the bad fortune each had brought to Dymchurch, wasted no words when Philip asked permission to marry Kate.

"No," he replied. "You will never have my permission, sir. I have noted your interest in my daughter, and hers in you. So I made it my business, sir, to learn something more about you than your military presence here. As a result, I now know your own family regards you as rebellious and independent. In fact, they have cut you off from the family fortune. Am I right?"

Philip bowed. "It is true, sir, that my father and I have—"

Sir Thomas cut in. "And you live on your Army pay. True?"

Again Philip nodded.

"Perhaps you are more interested in my daughter's fortune than in her hand," Sir Thomas said, coldly.

Philip's chin jutted out. "As Kate's father, sir, you may consider it your privilege to question my honor. I'm afraid I do not."

"Then I bid you good night, Mr. Brackenbury."

"Goodnight, Sir Thomas," Philip said stiffly, and turned on his heel.

In his haste to depart, he nearly knocked Kate off her feet at the door. "I'm leaving, Kate. After what your father said, there's nothing more to say. I'm sure you heard his words."

"Yes! And I heard yours, too!" Kate cried out sharply. "Only last night you said you would fight the world for me. The very next night I learn you would not fight even my father! Nothing more to say, indeed!"

"Oh, Kate!" Philip began. But at that moment, John came hurrying into the hallway. Without a word, he passed by them and on into his father's library.

Kate looked puzzled. "John looks as though he has seen a ghost."

Philip sighed. "And I'll wish I *were* one if the General sees me appear in the flesh much later than this. Kate, dear, I *will* speak to your father again. I know I can win him to our side."

But as Sir Thomas, with John, passed them in the hallway, Sir Thomas showed no sign of regretting his recent words. He ignored Philip. "Kate, isn't it your bedtime?" he asked sternly.

They went out the door.

"See?" Philip said gloomily. "The stars are just not right for us this evening, my dearest Kate."

In the stables, Dr. Syn listened to Harry.

"You know, Vicar, when we are in port, the Navy herds us below deck like cattle. We're fed, watered—yes. So that we may live for future slaughter on the high seas, I suppose. We—"

Sir Thomas, followed by John, strode through the doorway. "Vicar! John! Whatever is this mystery?"

Harry rose from the bale of hay on which he had been resting. "Hello, Father," he said quietly.

"Harry!" Sir Thomas' face went white. "It can't be you!" He rushed forward and clasped his eldest son in his arms. "I—I thought you were dead," he choked. "Dead!"

"Only half-dead," Harry replied, trying to smile.

"But son!" Sir Thomas looked and *was* dazed. "I don't understand. Why are you here, hiding like a criminal?"

"I *am* a criminal, sir."

Sir Thomas so bewildered, and Harry so weak, Dr. Syn took charge. "Harry's the Naval deserter they're looking for, Sir Thomas."

"You deserted?" Sir Thomas asked blankly.

"I escaped, Father. They took me by force. I got away by force. Four years of my life they've had."

Suddenly, he pulled at his shirt and lifted it high

on his back. "See, Father? Here are the decorations I got in the King's service."

Sir Thomas sank down onto the bale of hay. His eyes stared in shock.

"I'm no longer going to be treated this way," Harry said bitterly. "Not even for my King."

Sir Thomas stood up. "Of course, of course. Come to the house, lad. You must have food—care."

"He can't go there, Father," John said. "Our house will be searched. You heard the general. 'Spare no one,' he said."

"That's right," Sir Thomas said helplessly. "What can we do? Where can we hide him?"

"Leave that to me, Sir Thomas," Dr. Syn said. "Ask no questions, sir. If you know nothing, then you'll have nothing to hide when the Navy searching parties come. Please go into the house, sir. You too, John. Everything must appear as normal as possible."

Sir Thomas nodded. "You are right, of course, Vicar." He pressed Harry's hand. "I'll see you again, lad—soon, I know."

Philip Brackenbury mounting his horse, glanced in the direction of the stables, as Sir Thomas and John came up to the manor house. A puzzled look came over his face. "Goodnight, sirs," he said politely, and rode off.

"Do you think he saw anything, John?" Sir Thomas asked worriedly.

"I don't know, Father. But don't you worry. I'm going back to warn Dr. Syn. We'll get Harry away *very* soon."

CHAPTER 8

The vicar was glad enough to see John return. It had become plain that he would need help in getting Harry into the pony cart.

"Where are we taking him?" John asked anxiously.

"We?" the vicar repeated. "John, you must take no part in this. It is too dangerous!"

91

John didn't look as though he'd even heard Dr.
Syn speak. "We must leave for *somewhere* at
once!" he exclaimed. "Sooner or later Philip is sure
to remember that Harry was press-ganged. Then if
he thinks about seeing Father and me coming from
the stables—"

Dr. Syn was as worried as John. He frowned.
"With all Dymchurch in an uproar, Simon Bates
is in as much danger as Harry. And loyal Mrs.
Waggett will certainly be seized if the American is
discovered in the inn attic."

Harry, near collapse, had sunk to the stable
floor, his shoulders propped against the bale of
hay. "Don't worry longer," he said weakly. "You
saw Father's shock. It will kill him if I am discovered here. Please—just put me out on the marshes.
What matters? I feel like a dead man already."

"Dead man?" John repeated. He snapped his
fingers. "The very place! The graveyard! Vicar,"
he said briskly. "Harry—and Simon Bates, too—
can be fed, warm, and safe."

"Where, John?" Dr. Syn's voice almost shook.

"In the graveyard," John answered cheerfully.
"That is to say—in my family's crypt, the burial
vault. No one would think of searching there—not
even our eager General Pugh. Now come. Let's
get Harry into the cart."

With help, Harry was settled on the floor of the
little pony cart. "You'll ride in style, Harry," John
smiled. "Cheer up! No one will be even curious

about seeing the vicar returning home after a fine evening at the manor house!"

At the vicarage, Dr. Syn stopped only long enough to snatch up warm quilts. John, meantime, was sent to the sexton's house nearby, to rouse Mipps and send him to Mrs. Waggett's inn.

Then, on foot, the two helped Harry along the dark lane that led to the graveyard.

Despite his cheerful words, it was hard for John to feel that a graveyard vault was much of a place to leave his long-lost brother.

Once inside the stone building, a gust of chill, dank air struck their nostrils. Dr. Syn closed the heavy door. "Light the lantern, John. Keep the flame low."

Harry looked around at the rows of stone caskets, some with carved figures resting atop them. "My family!" he muttered. "Hundreds of years of proud history. I wonder what they'd think if they could see me here now? Running away like a stray dog!"

"They'd think you had good sense," Dr. Syn said. He flung a quilt over a coffin. "Now stretch yourself out here, lad. You'll sleep safe. And do not think beyond that. You'll soon have a roommate—Simon Bates, an American. We hope Mipps will be arriving with him any minute." He covered Harry with a second quilt. "Then before you know it, you lads will be safe out of here. I promise you."

John patted his brother's arm. "And the vicar always keeps a promise, I know that. Maybe—"

He broke off as a low knock sounded on the door.

"Mipps already!" said the vicar. "Cover the lantern, John." He opened the door. "All well, Sexton?" he asked sharply.

"All well, Vicar," Mipps answered. "Though I got him out none too soon. I daresay it was not five minutes before the troopers came to search the inn."

The vicar closed the door behind the two newcomers. John uncovered the lantern. Mipps eyes went to the quiet figure lying on the coffin top. "Mr. Harry, sir! I'd not have known you. It's good to see you, sir!"

For the first time, Harry grinned. "Better *on* than *in* one of your coffins, Sexton." Weakly, he held out his hand in greeting.

"Harry, this is Simon Bates," Dr. Syn said. "He too, is hunted by the Law."

"Naval deserter?" Harry asked as Simon took his hand.

"Worse," Simon grinned. "*England* deserter, you might say. I'm sentenced for preaching sedition—wanting freedom for the Colonies."

"And do you?" Harry asked.

"Guilty!" came the reply. "Only I didn't know it was a hanging crime to say so."

Dr. Syn stepped forward. "Harry, you'll remember Broken Barn in the Bonnington Hills?"

Harry nodded.

"You'll find horses there for your escape. To-morrow night you lads must go there and hide until I send word that the coast is clear."

"I could take them, Vicar," Mipps said.

"No. Remember—things must appear normal around here. The lads will have to go on their own. Right now, I should be in the vicarage and John at the manor house. Mind the lantern when we open the door. Goodnight, now, lads. You shall be brought food in the morning."

Mipps gave Harry and Simon instructions on the best way to get to Broken Barn. "Mr. Harry, enter through the barn doors. Under the fourth beam is a trap door leading to an underground stable."

"Underground stable!"

Mipps nodded. "That's right. You'll be perfectly safe there until it's time to flee. We'll get food to you. But whatever you do, *stay under cover!*"

"You and the vicar are taking a big risk." Harry said.

"So are you," Mipps replied seriously. He piled quilts on a second coffin for Simon. And within moments, the two fugitives of the law were left to enjoy as best they could, a night's rest in the Dymchurch graveyard.

Back in the vicarage, Mipps spoke frankly to Dr. Syn. "There are soldiers and pickets everywhere, Vicar. And those lads can't live forever underground. How ever will you get them to safety?"

"By the first ship that delivers for the Scarecrow. They must ride to the beach," Dr. Syn replied.

"You hope," said the sexton gloomily.

"I do," Dr. Syn said coolly. "And hope is brightest when it dawns from dark fear!"

By the time it was dark enough to set out for Broken Barn, Harry Banks and Simon Bates knew a great deal about each other's lives.

With food, rest, and an eagerness to leave their strange, gloomy haven, each felt almost fearless as they carefully opened the crypt door. The night air was damp, chilly—but fresh.

"Remember, Simon. No talking after we start," Harry whispered. "We don't want to be jumped by the King's men."

Simon couldn't agree more. "Will we follow a road?" he whispered.

"No. We'll cut cross-country. But there may be barking dogs along the way. I can't remember where each of my father's tenants live, but I'll try to keep clear of the cottages. Come on."

The first long mile passed in utter silence. Carefully, Harry led the way, keeping to the shadows and warning Simon in whispers of fallen tree-trunks and low-lying branches.

It was another half-hour before Harry stopped at a low stone wall and pointed ahead. "There it is," he whispered. "Over past the castle ruins—Broken Barn."

Simon could see how it had gained that name. Even in dim starlight, it had a dismal, deserted look. "I'll feel better once we reach that fourth beam the sexton spoke of," he whispered. "I have an awfully uneasy feeling, Harry."

"I guess anybody chased from here to there gets that feeling. But come on, Simon. Over the wall we go—then *safety*."

They had reached the shadow of the barn wall when the worst happened.

A pistol shot rang out. "HALT! in the King's name!"

Slowly, two pairs of arms raised in surrender.

"We're done for now," Harry groaned.

"Look's it," said the American briefly.

It was morning when Harry and Simon were led in chains along the streets of Dymchurch toward military headquarters.

Not all of the villagers saw them pass as the hour was early. But Mipps and his friend, Sam, were two who did.

"Mipps!" Sam gasped. "The first one there! That's Sir Harry's son or I miss my guess!"

The pair were pulled and dragged to the entrance of the headquarters.

"What's this?" asked the guard at the door.

"We caught the deserter and another one besides," came the triumphant reply.

The guard flung open the door. "Call off the search, Corporal. We have 'em!" he shouted.

The door closed behind the chained pair—but not before Mipps saw the corporal stride up and strike Simon across the face.

A sick feeling came over him. "Oh, it will be hard, hard news for the vicar!" he muttered.

"What's that you said, Mipps?" asked Sam.

"Hard news for Sir Thomas," Mipps answered. "I'd best let the vicar tell him. Good day, Sam. I've no heart for what I have to do."

Shoulders drooping, he paced back along the street, and turned in the long lane that led to the vicarage.

As Mipps was walking away, Simon and Harry were already realizing how terrible their future would be.

"Once again," the corporal grated out. "Who are you?"

Neither answered.

The corporal stood up. "You'll find your tongues, I promise you."

He looked from one to the other. "You're going to be sorry you were ever born—the pair of you!" He motioned to the guards. "Take them off. They are to go to Dover Castle immediately."

Dover Castle! Simon Bates knew it well. Dover Castle *prison*—and a dungeon prison at that.

They dared not look at each other. Neither

wanted the other to glimpse the despair that must show in their eyes.

In the long hours that passed before the newest prisoners in the dungeon were to be hauled up before General Pugh, Simon and Harry saw enough misery around them to last a long lifetime. Guilty or innocent, the men who shared the dark dungeon room, seemed to have lost all hope of living.

Some were quiet, gaunt men, so weakened by imprisonment that they barely looked up when Simon and Harry were flung to the hay-strewn dungeon floor. Others pulled at their shackles and raged at the guards. These were the younger men, caught wherever they might have been when the Navy gangs roamed the streets of Dover in search of "sailors." " 'Slaves,' more likely," Harry muttered. "Poor fellows."

Hours passed. "Is it day or night, do you think?" Simon asked.

Harry sat up. "Must be night. Simon tell me—what is it like in the American Colonies? Very different than England, I suppose."

Simon sighed. "I saw very little of your England. And if you can believe it, Harry, though I was born in the Colonies, before coming here I thought of it as 'my England.' "

"If you felt that way, then why did you wish to separate from it?"

"I didn't. Not when I first came. I wanted the Government to understand why we Colonials believe it unjust to pay taxes yet have no representation from the Colonies in Parliament. But now——." Simon shrugged. "I think it *is* time for the Colonies to form a new nation. England doesn't seem fair even to Englishmen."

"England isn't just King George," Harry said loyally. "Times will change one of these days."

"Not soon enough for us, I fear," Simon muttered. He sighed again. "Anyhow, I failed in my mission and I'll die for it. But Harry, I swear to you—I'll be dying for my *own* country—*a new land across the sea*!"

There was a long silence. Then Harry whispered, "I love England. But no one will believe I deserted only a cruel system. They'll think of me as a traitor."

"Cheer up, mate," Simon said wearily. He reached out and pressed Harry's arm. "*We* know we're true men, and—and—"

"And all that," Harry barely whispered as he drifted off to sleep.

CHAPTER 9

In the morning, Harry and Simon were shoved and dragged before General Pugh by a jailer. The general stared icily at the dirty, miserable pair who stood shackled in front of him. Philip Brackenbury sat at one side of the desk.

The general put his fingertips together. "Bates, and whoever *you* are, you miserable deserter—you'll give me the information I want here

101

and now, or I'll hand you over to more forcible persuasion."

He leaned back. "I could have you both hanged today, you know. Both of you are already condemned. But turn King's evidence, and I'll spare your lives. Now then—*who sheltered you all this time?*"

Neither Harry nor Simon spoke.

"It was this Scarecrow who flouts the law down there in Dymchurch, wasn't it?"

"No," Harry answered.

"Then one of his men?" asked the general. "Answer me!"

"No." Harry replied firmly.

"Then why did you head for these parts? You thought to get help from the Scarecrow, didn't you? You knew he'd helped other scoundrels to escape the King's law, didn't you?"

"No."

General Pugh stood up. "Talk, and I'll exchange your lives for theirs."

There was stone-solid silence.

"Very well." General Pugh strode to the door. "Jailer! Take these prisoners to the dungeons and see what answers you can get—and by whatever means."

Philip Brackenbury's face turned white. He stared down at his polished boots as the general turned to him.

"Well, Mr. Brackenbury, now you will see what I meant when I gave my definition of a good sol-

dier. Results! And that's what I mean to get." He looked sharply at his aide. "What's the matter Mr. Brackenbury. Not feeling too well, are you?"

There was a loud rap on the door.

"Enter." General Pugh shouted out.

A sentry stepped in. "The Vicar of Dymchurch to see you sir."

Dr. Syn, followed by John Banks, walked in. "Good day, General, Mr. Brackenbury." The vicar bowed.

General Pugh frowned. "Good day. Well, what do you want here, Parson?"

"On my duties, General. I'm chaplain to the jail. I've come to serve Holy Communion to the prisoners. And, as is customary, I am reporting to you first as garrison commander."

The general nodded. "And Master Banks?"

"He is here to assist me, sir."

General Pugh shrugged. "Well, it's not a duty I'd relish myself. The stench in the dungeon is strong enough to build another wall."

"Our duties are not always made easy—for any of us," the vicar nodded.

General Pugh granted. "But the end justifies the means, eh, Vicar?"

"Even when those means include torture, General?" Philip Brackenbury suddenly asked.

General Pugh grinned. "Mr. Brackenbury speaks of those swine who just left my quarters. Perhaps you saw them in the outer hall?"

The vicar nodded. "We noted them. Yes. But they are to be tortured, you say?"

"Certainly. They hold the key to unlock the conspiracy of silence that protects the Scarecrow madman. And I intend to get that key, Vicar. It is my duty."

Philip Brackenbury spoke again. "Tell me, General—when you promised them their lives if they told whatever they might know, would you have kept your side of the bargain?"

General Pugh burst into loud laughter. "My aide is a fool, is he not, Parson?" He looked coldly at Philip. "They'd hang anyhow, Mr. Brackenbury."

Philip turned even paler. "Of course, sir," he said, trying to keep his voice cool.

Dr. Syn bowed. "With your permission, sir, I'll go to the dungeons now. Your servant, sir."

As the vicar and John followed the jailer, Dr. Syn spoke in a low voice. "John, I need an ally here, and I think perhaps I've found one."

"Who?" John whispered.

"Philip Brackenbury."

At that moment, they reached the dungeon door. The jailer took out a heavy key and turned the lock. "Wake up in here!" he roared. "On your feet! Show some respect to the chaplain, you dogs!"

After the prisoners had staggered or lurched to

their feet, he left, leaving a guard standing inside the door.

By the guttering light of one melting candle, Dr. Syn looked at the poor fellows before him. "Kneel," he said softly. "Lift up your hearts in hope and trust. Let us pray."

Before prayers could begin, there was a shout from outside. "Open up! Naval picket."

Prisoners backed away in fright. The Navy press-gang!

In stepped a petty officer, followed by his men. "By your leave, Reverend. I am here to take six men."

He brushed by Dr. Syn. One by one, he chose six unfortunates. "Come on," he shouted. "Step lively if you don't want a mop's end broken across your backs." He called to his men. "Get them chained."

"Press-ganged!" Dr. Syn muttered. "Poor, poor fellows!"

The petty officer shouted orders. "You'll board the lugger for H. M. S. *Defiant*. Wave your mates goodbye, you dogs. We'll make men of you yet!"

Before the sad group could reach the door, two jailers entered carrying Harry and Simon. They slung them down like heavy sacks. "You obstinate rubbish! We haven't finished with you yet!"

The petty officer grinned at the jailers. "Here we are again, mates," he greeted them. "And here we go. Six less mouths for you to feed. MARCH!"

As the prisoners stumbled forward and filed by Dr. Syn, he spoke to them all. "God be with you and have mercy on you."

He stepped up to a jailer. "I am about to conduct a service here, jailer. I would like to be alone with the prisoners."

"But it ain't safe, your reverence," the jailer replied in shocked tones.

"Let me be the judge of that. Leave us."

The second the door closed, John was kneeling at Harry's side. His brother looked up at him, eyes clouded in pain. "They didn't make us talk," he mumbled.

Simon looked up. "Hello, Vicar," he said weakly. "We ran out of luck, didn't we?"

The vicar's face was pale. "Get up, John," he ordered. "The rest of you kneel again, and *listen to me.*"

He clasped his hands as though in prayer, then in a low voice spoke to the men bending before him. "Does the Naval picket come and go like that to take men to ships?"

The kneeling men murmured back. "Yes, sir. We never know when they'll come."

The vicar stared down at his clasped hands. "Harry, Mr. Bates, all of you—I don't know by what means, but somehow I'm going to get you away—all of you—before Pugh breaks your spirit as well as your body."

"There's no way out of here except in a coffin. Not for us," Simon Bates said.

"There will be. Trust me. All of you. I *will* get you free."

"*Free!*" voices rang out.

"Hush!" said the vicar. "Repeat after me." He began a prayer.

The jailer opened the door. Hearing a prayer in progress, he hung the key on a nail and stepped outside again.

"Men, keep on praying," Dr. Syn ordered. His voice dropped low. "John, take that key by the door. Drip hot wax on it from that candle on the table, quickly!"

A mold of the dungeon key! John instantly understood.

It seemed to the jailer standing outside, that the vicar of Dymchurch was conducting an extra-long service. He shrugged. "If he can stand that room, I guess I can stand his praying," he muttered. He waited. In a very short time the vicar and John came out the door.

"You're a good man, Vicar," he said raspingly. "Them in there ain't worth your time. Hopeless cases, they be."

Dr. Syn nodded solemnly. "It is the hopeless most in need of hope, jailer. Thank you for the time you gave them."

The vicar had barely finished his evening meal when Mipps came in holding a heavy key in his hand.

"It's pretty good, sir," he said, putting the key

on the table. "Although I say it myself—pretty good."

"I hope it works," Dr. Syn said, "It's not *only* a key, Mipps. It's a key to the whole plan."

"What plan, sir?"

Dr. Syn looked up and smiled. "The Vicar of Dymchurch can't tell you. But the Scarecrow will, and he'll tell you within the hour at Five-Mile Barn. Curlew is already there with our men, so be off at once."

Mipps looked at the vicar worriedly. "One of these days, he's going to dare too much," he thought. "I wonder what's going on in that clever brain of his?"

"Well, Mipps, come now!" The vicar arose from the table. "Time runs out. On your way. Scarecrow will meet you there."

"And Hellspite will be waiting," Mipps sighed. "Off I go, sir."

It was black-dark when Scarecrow climbed up to the old barn loft where Hellspite and Curlew waited. He glowered down on his band of smugglers. "All here?" he called.

Sam, Mipp's friend answered. "All who was asked."

Scarecrow's frightening glance went from man to man. "Very well. Listen carefully. A shipment is due from Holland tomorrow night."

A pleased murmur swept the crowd. Scarecrow's arm shot up. "Silence! We will *not* be taking cargo."

There was dead quiet among the smugglers.

"Instead," Scarecrow continued, "we shall be taking the *ship*."

"The ship!" the startled cry went up.

Scarecrow nodded his hideous head. "I have business—*export* business. That means we shall be sending out cargo, not bringing it in. Hellspite will tell each man his task. I shall say only this. There are prisoners in Dover Castle. They need my help. I intend to release them."

Scarecrow's men were stunned. Loyal though they were, it was one thing to ride the marshes at night. It was quite another to ride to dreaded Dover Castle.

Sam spoke for them all. "Release prisoners from those *dungeons,* sir? However can we do that?"

"By following a plan," Scarecrow said harshly. "Twelve of our men will meet and board the Dutchman's ship. They'll offer him gold to sail her into St. Margaret's bay, this side of Dover. Two men will stay aboard. Two men each will bring two small boats ashore. The remaining six will report to Hellspite at Dymchurch graveyard." He leaned forward. "You—Sam. Remember for all—eight o'clock tomorrow night is the hour."

Then he looked out across the upturned faces. "Ben Davis," he called. "You and others will be needed in entering the Castle dungeon. You will be led by the Vicar of Dymchurch, Dr. Syn."

"The vicar!" All the men gasped.

"Why's that?" Ben Davis called out.

"He's under my orders," Scarecrow cried hoarsely. "He has no choice. With him will be the squire's son, John. I have proof that those two gave shelter to a deserter from the Navy. If they refuse to help me, this proof will be handed to General Pugh. They know this. Refusal to help will mean they hang."

"Hang the *vicar*!" Ben gasped. "Blackmail *him*?"

Scarecrow looked fiercely down at them all. "To keep my word to those who are promised help, I'd blackmail the King himself!"

There was a long silence.

"Then the plan is set?" Scarecrow swung down from the loft, cloak swirling. "Ben Davis. You trust me?"

Ben nodded.

"Do all of you?" demanded Scarecrow. "Stand forward now and say if you are afraid."

"I ain't afraid," Sam called out from the crowd.

"Nor me," Ben Davis said. "But somehow—the vicar, Scarecrow! He's been a good friend to all us farmers."

"Leave Dr. Syn to me," Scarecrow answered. "Harm will come to me before it comes to him. That I promise you. *And you know Scarecrow keeps his promises*."

He clenched his fist. "Now Scarecrow and his

Gentlemen will give General Pugh's nose not a tweak but a twist. And such a twist as it never felt. And that goes for the King's injustice, too! Are you with me lads?"

"Aye!" voices rose.

Scarecrow only glared. "Remember! You are all to meet at the graveyard. On *time*! At eight, exactly. Hellspite will tell you how we will storm Dover Castle."

Then, cloak flowing, he strode from Five-Mile Barn, leaving a stunned crowd of farmers-turned-smugglers behind him.

CHAPTER 10

A waning moon shone palely down on low-lying ground fog. And in that rolling mist, the smugglers made their way in and around old tomb-
stones toward the church.

Mipps and John were last to arrive. As they
turned into the graveyard, the sexton, wearing his
Hellspite mask, took out a pistol. "Now, don't fail
us, Master John. *Look* scared. Remember—you're

not Curlew tonight, but Master John Banks, the squire's son. You've never seen a smuggler before in your life!"

It wasn't hard for John to forget past adventures as Curlew. All he could think of was Harry's danger. He stumbled forward as Mipps prodded him in the back straight into the band of smugglers gathered by the wall.

Still holding the pistol on John, Mipps spoke to all.

"Gentlemen have—"

John burst in. "Who are these men?" he demanded. "Why have you brought me here? Are you the Scarecrow's band?"

Mipps began again. "Quiet! Gentlemen have already been assigned to take the ship. Now your orders are to get the press-gang uniforms. We ride to Mrs. Waggett's inn. There you'll find the Navy gang, and when you leave, not a single sailor will be wearing one. *You* will be."

"But why—" John began.

"Never you mind," Mipps growled. He handed a mask to John. "Put this on, young Master, and follow me. See that he does, Gentlemen, in the name of the Scarecrow!"

Business had never been better at Mrs. Waggett's.

With General Pugh safe off in Dover Castle, the Naval pickets were quick to see the advantage of a fine evening at the inn—and with no fear of the

General breathing fiery snorts on the necks of jolly Naval press-gangs!

From petty officer to drummer boy, the seamen were gathered together, merrily singing. And from outside the inn, Mipps and his masked band could clearly hear their roaring, rousing songs.

Beneath his mask, Mipps grinned. "They'll never know what hit them—or who!" he exclaimed gleefully. "But don't lay a hand on the drummer boy. Mrs. Waggett'll look after him. Young Master, looks to me you're going to be a mite tall for his uniform, but you'll be wearing it."

"*I!*" John exclaimed in a shocked voice.

"If you don't want to swing, you will," Mipps threatened. "We know who gave shelter to a deserter! Don't think we don't!"

"Now, come on, Gentlemen. *Rush them!*"

Mrs. Waggett said later, she'd never seen such an uproar in all her days of running the inn. "My wits about left me when that Scarecrow's gang slammed in through my door!" she told her friends. "Thump! Bang! Bump! Why, you couldn't see across the room for flying chairs and swinging fists! And tankards! My good tankards! Falling about like rain they were! It was terrible! Terrible!"

What Mrs. Waggett *didn't* say later, was one word about the tankard *she* threw.

As the smugglers burst in, she gave an extra-loud shriek of dismay and fright. Then snatching the drummer boy up by the collar, she circled him with one hefty arm. She dragged him, kicking and screaming across the room and took shelter in a doorway.

"Let me GO!" he yelled.

"Hush!" Mrs. Waggett shrieked back. "This is for your own good, my lad!" She reached out to a nearby table and grabbed a mug. "Take that!" she screamed, aiming at a Naval picket, but belting a smuggler square on the head.

"Mercy me!" she gasped in shock as one of her best customers sank to the floor. "This is no place for a lady."

But even without Mrs. Waggett's help, the fight was going in favor of the smugglers.

"Off with their uniforms," Mipps yelled. "And *don't* tear 'em!"

He seized the drummer boy. "You'll come to no harm, lad," he said. "Come now. Off with that uniform."

Mrs. Waggett shrieked modestly at these words.

"Upstairs, missus," Mipps ordered roughly. "Off you go!"

Mrs. Waggett gasped, "Mercy!" and headed for the privacy of the second floor chambers with Mipp's words ringing in her ears—"Tie the buzzards up!"

He turned to the staircase and roared after the departing Mrs. Waggett. "If you know what's good for you, missus, you'll stay up there the night. This inn is closed for business!"

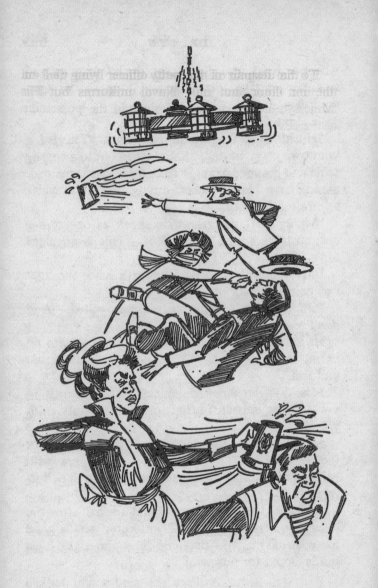

To the despair of the petty officer lying tied on the inn floor, not only Naval uniforms but His Majesty's horses, were no longer in the possession of the Royal Navy.

Outside, Mipps, still wearing his mask, tucked the petty officer's uniform under his arm and called, "Mount up, men! We're off to Dover Castle."

Then hoofbeats thundered away.

The thought of General Pugh's rage, and that of his own commander, was enough to make the helpless petty officer hope that he and his press-gang could remain on the inn floor forever!

Some time later, Dr. Syn, wearing that same unfortunate seaman's uniform, marched at the head of his "press-gang" to the gates of Dover Castle.

"Halt!" a sharp voice rang out. "Who goes there?"

Two guards at the gate stepped forward. At the same moment, Mr. Philip Brackenbury, out for a breath of night air and trying to get his mind off thoughts of torture, came into view.

Dr. Syns' heart sank. He hadn't thought of being seen by the general's aide. There was only one thing to do—answer in a brisk voice! "Naval picket for the pressed-men in the prison, sir."

Philip's ears pricked up. "I know that voice!" he muttered. He hesitated. Then taking a forward step, he said, "I'll escort them, guard."

Dr. Syn and the disguised smugglers, looked

straight ahead as they passed the guards and marched toward Philip Brackenbury.

"Forward!" shouted Mr. Brackenbury. His arm shot out and snatched John out of line. "Not you, powder-monkey! No need for a drummer boy where they're going! Back to the gates with you!"

John's heart thudded. "He must have seen who I was," he thought desperately. "He looked straight at me!" He watched, heart sinking, as Kate's beloved marched side-by-side with Dr. Syn across the long, cobblestone courtyard. "Did he keep me out because of Kate? Is he taking the vicar straight to General Pugh?" His thoughts raced. "There's nothing to do but wait it out!"

He watched, almost without breathing, as Dover Castle's heavy doors closed grimly on as true a band of men as were ever born on Romney Marsh.

At the door of the dungeon corridor, Philip Brackenbury ordered the press-gang to halt. "Two men step forward. Others, wait here," he commanded.

As this change in formation was made, he stepped ahead and whispered quickly to Dr. Syn. "What are you trying to do, sir?"

"Release the prisoners from injustice and torture," the vicar whispered back, not turning his head. "Isn't that what you want, too?"

"How will you open the dungeon?" Philip muttered.

"With this." Dr. Syn held up a key.

The two men stepped forward. And as Ben and Sam followed several paces behind the King's petty officer and Mr. Brackenbury, Ben Davis shook his head. "Even the vicar will hang if they catch us now with him dressed like that!"

Ahead of them, Mr. Brackenbury asked. "You have no official papers?"

"Not official. No."

"Quiet, then. Utmost quiet. We must pass the jailers' room."

The four men advanced along the dim, long corridor, lighted only with smoky, far-spaced torch flares. As they neared the jailers' room, voices could be plainly heard.

"Why don't you give up?" said one. "I've won the game anyhow."

"No, we'll play it out."

"Well, I've finished, anyway. And it's time to do the rounds."

"Aw, sit down. Come on. Let's play one more game. Start fresh. Your deal."

"*I* give the orders here."

"That you do. That you do. But you don't shuffle cards too well. Do you?"

"You saw me. It was a fair deal."

"Come on. Let me watch you again."

When only the clicking of cards could be heard, Philip motioned the group forward. The four passed the jailers' room and on to the dungeon door.

Dr. Syn gripped the heavy key in both hands.

"It *has* to work," he murmured, and bent forward.

Mipps had done his work well. The heavy door swung in.

"What was that?" came a voice from the jailers' room.

"Rat." the other laughed. "What's the matter? I deal too good to suit you?"

Again, there was silence.

Softly, Dr. Syn closed the door behind them. He hurried forward and shook awake the first huddled form he came to. "Keep quiet. I'm the vicar. Do as you're told. We'll get you away from here."

One by one, but swiftly, the prisoners were awakened.

Then Dr. Syn knelt by Harry and Simon. "Will you be able to walk, lads?" he asked anxiously.

Both nodded.

"Good lads!"

Other prisoners helped Harry and Simon to their feet. "Ready, mates?" one whispered.

"No noise," Dr. Syn muttered. "Not another word. We're going to have to chain you together so that crossing the courtyard, the guards will not become suspicious."

Shackling the prisoners made more noise than the loudest whisper, but it had to be done. Sam stood guard at the door. "Ssh!" he hissed.

"Down!" Dr. Syn ordered. Along with Philip Brackenbury, Sam and Ben, he pressed flat back

along the dark wall and the prisoners dropped back on the floor.

A tiny window in the door slid back and a lantern held up. The jailer was satisfied with what he saw. His footsteps grew faint.

"All right!" Dr. Syn whispered. "Now quickly. Quickly!"

As they opened the dungeon door, talk from the jailers' room floated out.

"What was it?"

"Nothing. The louts had probably been fighting. Believe me, they were lying there like lambs when they heard me come up!"

"Then let's get on with the game."

Then to the great relief of the Vicar of Dymchurch the jailers began to quarrel. Their voices rose higher.

"That was my trick!"

"It was mine!"

"*I* played the king."

"No you didn't. You played the jack."

"Are you calling me a liar?"

In the noisy squabble that followed, prisoners and rescuers made it safely down the long corridor and through the door.

"There's still the main door," Sam whispered.

"And that courtyard and the guards," Ben Davis whispered back. "Me heart's knocked me ribs through already."

Ben Davis's ribs were not the only ones that ached in fear. Still at his waiting post, John Banks watched the big doors anxiously. In the light of the torch flares at the entrance, one swung open. *Out stepped General Pugh!*

John pressed back into the deep shadow of the courtyard wall hardly daring to take the next aching breath. "If he sees me, we're all done for!" he groaned.

CHAPTER 11

Marching forward, hands clasped behind his red coat, the general strode to the exact middle of the courtyard. Then, as he came to a dead stop and gazed up at the faint stars, out came the "press-gang" escorted by his Majesty's Officer, Mr. Philip Brackenbury.

As one man, Philip and Dr. Syn saw the danger ahead! For a split second, Philip broke stride.

And in the same instant, the Vicar of Dymchurch bawled out loudly, "Fall in, men! We've got us a good haul this night for His Majesty's Navy!"

Philip Brackenbury took one deep breath. "Forward," he snapped out. Steadily he struck off across the cobblestones, straight toward the gates —and General Pugh."

"Halt!" the general bellowed. "What's this, Mr. Brackenbury?"

"Naval picket for the pressed-men, sir."

General Pugh grunted and turned to survey the situation for himself.

John Banks froze. For a moment, John forgot even Harry. The general was heading straight for the petty officer of the press-gang—the Vicar of Dymchurch!

"Straighten up, you mangy dogs," the general roared.

As nothing else could have, those cruel words seemed to spring young John back from his daze! *Harry or any one of those miserable men, a mangy dog!*

Furious, he began a loud, long rolling *rat-ta-tat-tat* on the drum and marched slowly forward.

General Pugh spun around. "Why's this boy out of line, Mr. Brackenbury?" he shouted.

"By my order, sir. I would not allow him within the Castle," Philip answered.

General Pugh stamped over to his aide. "And why not, may I ask? You considered him too young for such sights, I presume?" he asked icily.

"I did, sir," Mr. Brackenbury replied, staring straight ahead.

General Pugh sighed loudly. "Ah, Mr. Brackenbury!" he exclaimed in mock sorrow. "That the King's Navy men could hear that an officer of the King's Army thinks so tenderly makes me sad indeed!" His tone suddenly changed. "I'll deal with you later!" he grated out.

Then, forgetting he was a general and that there was any such thing as a chain of command, he swung back to the halted group. "You're in the King's Service now. *Quick* march!"

"Quick march!" Mr. Brackenbury echoed. He saluted. The salute was returned. And as the general retired to quarters in Dover Castle, Dr. Syn led his men and their bedraggled prisoners safely beyond the gates—John beating out a marching rhythm on his "borrowed" drum.

Once outside the gates, only the quick help of the prisoner chained beside him, kept Harry Banks from sliding to the ground.

Escape had been made—and none too soon!

In Sir Thomas' drawing-room, Kate turned away from her place at the harpsichord. "Father, I don't have the heart for one more tune."

Sir Thomas arose slowly from his chair by the fireside. "I know, dear. You've been a brave girl to play even one melody tonight. I know you grieve for Harry as much as I." He shook his head. "My boy—my *boy*—sent off in chains to prison!"

Kate's voice trembled. "Don't father—don't," she begged.

Sir Thomas turned and stared into the blazing flames licking around the logs. "I'd think young John would have had little zest for running off to wherever he runs to of nights. He's not a heartless lad. Yet how could he enjoy the company of his friends when he knows his own brother is doomed by King's law?"

Kate shook her head. "I cannot believe anything but good of John, Father. I don't believe he is—"

There was a sudden sound of a slamming door behind her. Mipps, wearing his Hellspite mask, entered the room flourishing a pistol.

"What in—" Sir Thomas gasped.

Mipps bowed. "Hellspite of The Gentlemen. At your service, sir."

"The *Gentlemen!* You smuggling scoundrels! What do you want in my house?" Sir Thomas thundered.

"You, squire. And your daughter."

"Why, you—"

"Quiet!" Mipps said sharply. "Quiet and easy, squire. No hollering out for servants, or my friends outside will have something to say. The Scarecrow needs you."

"The Scarecrow!"

"To act as hostage, squire, while he does a little business."

Kate and her father looked at each other in alarm.

"Come quiet, sir," Mipps urged. "You'll not be harmed." He flourished the pistol. "But make trouble and I'll blow your brains out. There's a carriage waiting in the lane. Now, not a word so no one gets hurt."

Kate huddled fearfully beside her father when they stepped outside the door of the manor house.

Not only was a carriage waiting, but a masked band of smugglers—the feared Gentlemen of the Marshes!

In a clump of trees near the shoreline of St. Margaret's bay, the Vicar of Dymchurch halted his sad group of prisoners.

"I was told to bring you only as far as here, then leave you. The one called "Scarecrow" will see that you get into the boats that await. Goodbye, lads, and God bless you all."

He turned his horse. "Hurry, John. The Scarecrow ordered that you be short in your leavetaking if you value your brother's life."

The prisoners stared after the galloping horse and rider, fast swallowed up in the gloom.

"This is a dream," muttered one.

"May I never awake from it!" said another.

John moved quickly to Harry's side. "You heard the vicar, Harry. I have to leave you."

Harry clutched his brother's arms. "You're a brave lad, John. Father must be very proud of you. Give him so much love from me, won't you?

And to Kate, too. How I wish I could have said goodbye to both!"

John swallowed. "Scarcely to have seen you!" he choked. "It is so unfair!"

Harry tried weakly to thump his young brother's shoulder. "At least you see me living," he smiled.

In the still night came the distant sound of hoofbeats and carriage wheels. John looked landward. "Goodbye, dear Harry. Goodbye all."

Swiftly, he too, rode away into darkness, leaving the men huddled and uncertain beneath the trees.

"Who comes?" One poor fellow whispered, fright in his voice as the distant sounds drew close.

"Not King's men," another answered. "Not in a carriage would *they* be."

But no matter what each had imagined, not one of the prisoners was prepared for the strange sight that came bursting out of the gloom. The Scarecrow! And at either side of the carriage behind him, the wildly masked figures of Hellspite and Curlew!

As the Scarecrow reined up the big iron-gray, a figure stood up in the carriage. Furious, Sir Thomas called out. "You—you *rogue!* What do you want with me and my daughter?"

Scarecrow dismounted. He bowed to the squire. "Sir Thomas, you'll thank me before this night is out!" said that dreadful apparition.

Then he turned to the dark clump of trees. "To

the beach, men," he cried out into the shadows. "Sir Thomas. Mistress Banks. Follow me!"

As he began to stride toward the beach, a voice from the huddled group called out, "Father!"

Sir Thomas looked unbelievingly into the shadows. "Harry? Harry? Is that you, lad?"

Harry stumbled forward. Sir Thomas sprang down from the carriage. With no help, Kate followed her father.

The Scarecrow strode to the water's edge where two small boats were pulled up on the sand and four masked men awaited. "Come!" he called. "Hurry!"

The prisoners moved forward as fast as they could. All but Harry Banks.

Sir Thomas, running, hugged his son close. "Harry! Harry! You're free! But how?"

From the beach, Scarecrow laughed hideously. "What say you now, Squire?"

Then, turning his back upon the Banks family, he strode up to a dark, sturdy figure standing by one of the boats. "Captain? Keep your cargo for another night. You have passengers to take aboard. Straight to Holland, sir." He flung out a money bag. "Here is your payment."

The Dutch captain felt the weight of the money bag and grinned. "As you say, Mynheer. The cargo can wait!"

The line of men had gathered on the sandy cove and the captain turned to them. "Hurry. Hurry! Into the boats! We must catch the tide!"

Sir Thomas scarcely heard the captain's words. "Kate," he cried to his daughter who stood wide-eyed beside him. "Your *brother!* Don't you remember Harry?"

Kate burst into tears. She flung her arms around the tall, tattered figure of her brother. "I do. I do! But, oh, Harry! When I heard Father call out your name, I thought he'd lost his mind from worry about you!"

Harry patted her. "There, there, now Kate—" He held her off a bit. "Why! My little sister's grown into a beauty!"

The Scarecrow loomed up. "Into the boat! You heard the captain. GO!"

But the Scarecrow's help was needed by Sir Thomas to get Harry the short distance from the trees to the boats. Then Scarecrow turned to the Dutchman. "Help these men to board a boat for America."

"America!" Simon Bates cried out.

Scarecrow roared with harsh laughter. "America! Now off with you! Mynheer, you're in enemy waters—you smuggling rogue!"

He clasped Sir Thomas' arm. "Time to go, Squire. My men will escort you home, sir." He bowed. "Your servant, sir."

"So short a time," Sir Thomas cried. "Goodbye, dear lad. Remember us!"

"Goodbye, Father! Kate!" Harry exclaimed chokingly.

Simon Bates, nearly as battered and bruised as

Harry, stepped forward. "Don't worry, sir. I'll take care of him. We'll get word to you somehow, too."

"Hurry! Get aboard!" Scarecrow urged. "There's a new life awaiting you, gentlemen!"

Cloak blowing, he waved as the two small boats shoved off. "A new world and freedom very soon. *BON VOYAGE!*"

CHAPTER 12

It was not until morning when a quivering jailer made his report, that the garrison commander had the least idea that, along with the others, his two prize prisoners were gone.

Hardly had he learned that dreadful fact, than a messenger from Mrs. Waggett of Dymchurch inn, was announced by the guard.

"I hardly know, sir," said the newcomer, bowing humbly, "whether I should be telling you, the general this. Or should I be telling the admiral, sir?" He bowed again. "I'm the Dymchurch cobbler, sir."

"I don't care who you are," General Pugh roared. "What are you talking about? Get on with it, man! Tell what?"

"Tell about what happened to poor Mrs. Waggett," the cobbler said. "Screaming out her window, she was, at dawn this morning, sir. Couldn't come downstairs because of the Naval picket, she said."

"And why not?" snapped the general furiously.

"Too much of a lady was Mrs. Waggett for that, sir." the cobbler answered. "They was tied up all over the place—naked you might say. Leastwise, they was lacking their uniforms. The Scarecrow's men it was, sir. Mrs. Waggett said it was terrible. Terrible." He blinked at the general. "I come straight to you, sir, soon's I heard the dreadful news."

General Pugh nearly choked on the sudden understanding of who last night's press-gang had been. Scarecrow's Gentlemen of the Marshes!

Scarecrow had outwitted him again!

As soon as the door closed on the cobbler, General Pugh bawled out to the miserable jailer. "Get Mr. Brackenbury in here. At once!" he shouted. "And get back here yourself. I'm not through with *you!*"

General Pugh had promised he would deal with

Mr. Brackenbury. But as things were turning out, the general had even more to say than he'd planned.

He paced angrily back and forth before Philip and the jailer. "And you suspected nothing when you took them to the dungeons, Mr. Brackenbury?"

Philip Brackenbury lifted his chin. "I had no reason, sir. They had release papers."

"Aaah!" General Pugh turned on the jailer. "So what then happened?"

The jailer quavered. "They—they didn't come to me for the key, sir. Neither did you, Mr. Brackenbury."

"But they had a key." Philip replied calmly.

General Pugh stared. "And that didn't seem strange to you, Mr. Brackenbury?"

"No, sir. I'm not familiar with jail procedure. The men's actions seemed routine to me."

"Dismissed!" General Pugh barked. "Wait outside the door."

The unlucky jailer shook as General Pugh stepped toward him. "You fool! Why didn't you see them or hear them? You were on duty. Were you fighting, sleeping—or what?"

"No. No, sir," the jailer gasped.

"Get out!"

"Yes sir, General, sir."

Alone, General Pugh paced the room. "Mr. Brackenbury," he bellowed.

As Philip Brackenbury opened the door, the general whirled on him. "You dunderhead! The deserter. The American. They had the answers to everything I wanted. Through them I'd have smashed the smuggling ring."

He paced back and forth. "Imposters walk into the Castle and out again with prisoners. And right under your very nose!"

"You saw them, too, sir," his aide replied steadily. "You were at the gate when they marched through."

He handed a folded paper to the general. "It's all in my report, sir. I sent a copy to the admiral by the evening post last night."

"To the *admiral*!"

Philip nodded. "Also a copy to the Director of Public Prosecutions, sir. I believe he makes his report to the King, does he not?"

"You know he does," General Pugh raged. "Thank you, Mr. Brackenbury. That was very thoughtful of you."

Philip Brackenbury stood still as a statue. "My duty, sir," he said in a hard voice.

General Pugh blazed as hot as Philip was cold. "Duty!" he exclaimed. "*Dismissed*!"

As Philip closed the door, the general sunk down at his desk. He held his aide's report to the light. "*General Pugh was at the gate.*"

"Finished! Finished!" he groaned aloud. "I will be relieved of my command!"

By noonday, Dr. Syn, back from his morning rounds of calls upon the villagers, gave Mipps the latest gossip in Dymchurch.

"Yes," he said, his eyes twinkling. "Mrs. Waggett's inn is open for business again. I understand the press-gang had to leave in borrowed sheets. And the cobbler told me that just before he left Dover after his call upon General Pugh, he heard it rumored that the general was taking the Royal Mail coach to London this very afternoon."

"I've news for you, too, Vicar." Mipps grinned. "You're invited to dine at the manor house tonight. Master John said his father has amazing news to tell you."

"And of course I must be very surprised when I hear it," Dr. Syn chuckled.

It was plain to Dr. Syn that Sir Thomas could hardly wait for the evening meal to end.

"You'll never believe it, Vicar. Never!" Sir Thomas exclaimed the moment a servant closed the drawing-room doors behind them.

John Banks listened quietly while his father told of the past night's strange events. But Kate scarcely raised her head. Harry's sad condition spelled the end to her dreams of Philip Brackenbury. Dover Castle and all it stood for were too terrible to think of. And Philip was a part of that cruel place.

Dr. Syn's glance went from Sir Thomas to John and then to Kate. He set down his cup. "This is indeed an amazing tale you tell me, Sir Thomas. Wonderful, indeed!"

Sir Thomas sighed. "Only one sad thing—John was not at home when the Scarecrow came." He glanced sternly at his youngest son. "Were it not your habit to constantly run off to goodness knows where, you'd have been able to bid your brother farewell."

John exchanged a quick glance with Dr. Syn. "It is enough to know Harry is safe, Father. My being there would have had no meaning."

The Vicar of Dymchurch arose. "John!" he exclaimed. "Clearly you have told your father nothing!"

John's dark eyes widened and flickered in amazement, and Sir Thomas looked from the vicar to his son. "What do you mean?" he asked slowly. "What—"

"Why, Sir Thomas!" Dr. Syn exclaimed. "Surely you have heard this day of the Scarecrow's raid on Mrs. Waggett's inn last night? Mipps tells me the dreadful story is all over the village."

Sir Thomas looked bewildered. "Yes, but what has that to do with John?"

"A great deal," Dr. Syn replied. "Village gossip has it that the Scarecrow forced John to put on the uniform of the press-gang's drummer boy. And it is said that had not Mr. Philip Brackenbury seized John by the collar and kept him from entering the Castle, he would have been with those other madmen."

Kate's eyes grew as large and amazed as her brother's. Sir Thomas turned pale. "Is this true, John?" he asked.

John nodded. Sir Thomas jumped to his feet. "That wretch! That Scarecrow! To have risked my boy's life in such a plot!"

"Which boy's life?" Dr. Syn asked quietly.

"John's, of course!" Sir Thomas exclaimed. "Do you think I'd have traded one son's life for the other's? I might have lost *both* my boys!"

"Certainly I thought no such thing," Dr. Syn replied. "But I do wonder—" He let his voice trail off.

"Wonder what?" Sir Thomas snapped.

"Well, the thought just now passed through my mind—Mr. Philip Brackenbury must be badly in need of spectacles, wouldn't you say?"

Sir Thomas looked puzzled. "I don't follow your thoughts, Vicar. In any case, I care little whether that young man needs spectacles or not."

Dr. Syn shrugged. "I daresay. Yet it does seem strange, does it not, that he plucked John from the others? Almost seems as though he wanted no harm to come to him, doesn't it?"

Before Sir Thomas could reply, a knock sounded at the drawing-room doors and a servant stepped in.

"Mr. Philip Brackenbury to see Sir Thomas, sir," he said.

Sir Thomas hesitated. "Show him in," he ordered.

"Now not a word about this," Dr. Syn whispered warningly. "We can run no risks with a King's Officer!"

As he entered, Philip bowed briefly to Kate, then to the others. "I'll state my errand now and before all, Sir Thomas," he said. "I again ask permission for Kate's hand. When last I spoke, you objected to my Army pay in supporting your daughter. Now I must tell you, I do not have even that to offer. I am resigning my commission. I say only that I have faith in a new future, wherever it may be, if Kate is by my side."

There was a silence so deep and long that Kate could not bear it. She moved swiftly to Philip.

"And I wish to be at Philip's side, Father."

A sudden faint smile twitched Sir Thomas' lips. "I shall have to think this over, Mr. Brackenbury. Tell me—do you see clearly?"

Philip looked puzzled.

"I mean, of course, do you see the *future* clearly?" Sir Thomas added.

"No sir. I must admit I do not. But I *feel* my actions to be right."

"Ah. Very good." Sir Thomas smiled. He waved his arm toward a sofa across the room. "Pray, Kate. Show our guest to a comfortable seat."

Philip and Kate were soon murmuring in low voices, almost unaware there were others in the room. Kate's eyes glowed happily. "If only Harry were here, everything would be perfect!"

Philip pressed her hand. "You may see him sooner than you think, Kate dear."

"Oh, Philip! No! He must not come back. It would mean his death!"

Philip smiled. "We *both* may see him soon."

"You mean—America?" Kate whispered.

"A new life. A new country," Philip whispered back.

Across the room Dr. Syn arose. "Well, Sir Thomas, I'll say it again—this is a strange story you have told me. But—er—scoundrel or no, this Scarecrow fellow freed Harry and made it possible for you to say farewell." He paused. "As parson and squire, we must hope for his capture, but—er—tonight let's drink to him, shall we?"

"Ah, well—I suppose so," Sir Thomas replied.

"And let's toast the young people, too. He's a good lad, you'll see."

"There's another good lad in this room. That I *know*." Sir Thomas said seriously. "This is a happy night for us all!"

The squire arose. "A toast!" he called out. "To Philip, to Kate, and to—ah, the Scarecrow fellow!"

John's eyes sparkled. "Yes! To the Scarecrow! Whoever and wherever he may be—the scoundrel!"

Dr. Syn beamed. "The *scoundrel*!" he chuckled, lifting his glass.